For years Rachel had held off searching for Megan, telling herself that her daughter was happy. Safe. Loved.

What right did Rachel have to try to reclaim what she had relinquished? What right did she have to disrupt her daughter's life?

For years she had tried to ignore the longing, and for years she had failed. But then the dreams began, and her longing took on a life of its own. Something real, something human began to call out to her. When the dreams began to warn her of danger, she embarked on a mission to find her daughter.

And now the search was over.

She pulled out a photo of Megan and her adoptive father. She had to admit that Adam Wessler was handsome, in a chiseled sort of way. His strong, masculine face suggested fairness and integrity, but was it a kind face? A compassionate face? For her daughter's sake, she hoped it was.

Dear Reader,

As you ski into the holiday season, be sure to pick up the latest batch of Silhouette Special Edition romances. Featured this month is Annette Broadrick's latest miniseries, SECRET SISTERS, about family found after years of separation. The first book in this series is *Man in the Mist* (#1576), which Annette describes as "...definitely a challenge to write." About her main characters, Annette says, "Greg, the wounded lion hero—you know the type—gave me and the heroine a very hard time. But we refused to be intimidated and, well, you'll see what happened!"

You'll adore this month's READERS' RING pick, *A Little Bit Pregnant* (SE#1573), which is an emotional best-friends-turned-lovers tale by reader favorite Susan Mallery. *Her Montana Millionaire* (SE#1574) by Crystal Green is part of the popular series MONTANA MAVERICKS: THE KINGSLEYS. Here, a beautiful socialite dazzles the socks off a dashing single dad, but gets her own lesson in love. Nikki Benjamin brings us the exciting conclusion of the baby-focused miniseries MANHATTAN MULTIPLES, with *Prince of the City* (SE#1575). Two willful individuals, who were lovers in the past, have become bitter enemies. Will they find their way back to each other?

Peggy Webb tantalizes our romantic taste buds with *The Christmas Feast* (SE#1577), in which a young woman returns home for Christmas, but doesn't bargain on meeting a man who steals her heart. And don't miss *A Mother's Reflection* (SE#1578), Elissa Ambrose's powerful tale of finding long-lost family...and true love.

These six stories will enrich your hearts and add some spice to your holiday season. Next month, stay tuned for more page-turning and provocative romances from Silhouette Special Edition.

Happy reading!

Gail Chasan
Senior Editor

Please address questions and book requests to:
Silhouette Reader Service
U.S.: 3010 Walden Ave., P.O. Box 1325, Buffalo, NY 14269
Canadian: P.O. Box 609, Fort Erie, Ont. L2A 5X3

A Mother's Reflection

ELISSA AMBROSE

SPECIAL EDITION™

Published by Silhouette Books

America's Publisher of Contemporary Romance

For Bubbins.

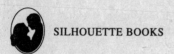

SILHOUETTE BOOKS

ISBN 0-373-24578-5

A MOTHER'S REFLECTION

Copyright © 2003 by Elissa Harris Ambrose

Printed in U.S.A.

Books by Elissa Ambrose

Silhouette Special Edition

Journey of the Heart #1506
A Mother's Reflection #1578

ELISSA AMBROSE

Originally from Montreal, Canada, Elissa Ambrose now resides in Arizona with her husband, her smart but surly cat and her sweet but silly cockatoo. She's the proud mother of two daughters, who, though they have flown the coop, still manage to keep her on her toes. She started out as a computer programmer and now serves as the fiction editor at *Anthology* magazine, a literary journal published in Mesa, Arizona. When she's not writing or editing or just hanging out with her husband, she can be found at the indoor ice arena, trying out a new spin or jump.

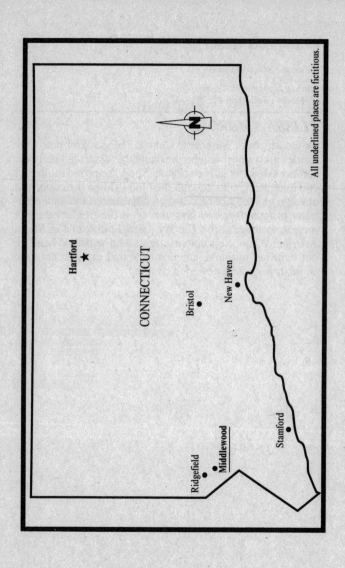

All underlined places are fictitious.

ACT ONE

Chapter One

Middlewood, 50 Miles.

The sign on the highway flashed by. Fifty miles to her future. Less than an hour away.

Rachel glanced at the speedometer, resisting the urge to press down on the accelerator. What was the hurry? What difference would another few minutes make? She'd already waited twelve years—twelve long, painful years. If not for the dreams, she would have been content to let the years become a lifetime.

No, not content. Resigned.

She gripped the steering wheel tightly as she recalled the private investigator's five simple words. Five simple words that had changed her life forever.

They lived in Middlewood, Connecticut.

So close.

How could she not have known? How could she not have felt it?

An hour and a half after leaving Hartford, she checked into the Colonial Inn. Her room with adjoining bath was cozy in charming New England–style, but it was out of her price range. She knew she would have to find an apartment soon, something small and reasonably priced. The P.I. had been expensive, and she was still paying rent in Hartford. Of course, if her plan succeeded, she wouldn't need the apartment in Hartford. She'd be living here in Middlewood.

After unpacking, she freshened up and changed into her green linen suit. She wanted to look professional yet feminine. Striking but not too brassy. First impressions lasted a lifetime, and a lifetime was what she was after.

She checked her watch. She still had half an hour. Sitting at the desk, she opened her briefcase. She picked up the large manila envelope and pulled out a photograph.

The girl in the picture, with those long lashes and high, angular cheekbones, might appear delicate to someone else, but Rachel wasn't fooled. The longer she stared at the glossy black-and-white image, the more the girl's nature seemed to emerge. Shoulder-length hair, clustering in curls around a heart-shaped face, made her look fragile, but the eyes, hard and direct, gave her away. "I dare you," they seemed to say. "I dare you to know me."

Rachel smiled to herself. She'd always said that when she had a baby, she would name her Katie. Katie Mc-Carthy, Rachel's grandmother, had been a willful and proud woman who had never turned down a challenge.

Rachel had handled the picture so many times these past few days, she was surprised that the finish hadn't worn away. "Katie," she whispered, tracing the outline of her daughter's face. Rachel had been seventeen when she'd given her up, twelve years ago. The adoption had been closed, the records sealed. According to the report, they'd named her Megan.

For years Rachel had held off searching for her, telling herself that her daughter was happy. Safe. Loved. What right did Rachel have to try to reclaim what she had relinquished? What right did she have to disrupt her daughter's life?

For years she had tried to ignore the longing, and for years she had failed. It had become as much a part of her as breathing. But then the dreams began, and her longing took on a life of its own. Something real, something human, began to call out to her, no louder than a whisper, as plaintive as a song on the wind. When the dreams began to warn her of danger, she embarked on a mission to find her daughter.

And now the search was over.

She pulled out another photo. She had to admit that Adam Wessler, Megan's adoptive father, was handsome, in a chiseled sort of way. His strong, masculine face suggested fairness and integrity, but was it a kind face? A compassionate face? For her daughter's sake, she fervently hoped it was.

Megan was being raised without a mother.

Once again Rachel checked her watch. It was time to go. She returned the photographs to the envelope, then picked up her purse and briefcase and left the inn.

The weather forecast had called for rain. She'd planned on driving, but once outside she decided to walk. The sky was luminously blue, without a cloud as far as she could see.

It wasn't the threat of rain that scared her.

One summer. She had almost three months to become an integral part of Megan's life. Only after she'd achieved this would she reveal her identity—and what kind of man would turn his back on someone who'd become so important to his daughter?

But what if he did? What if, once her secret was known, Adam shut her out?

Another worry assailed her, this one more pressing. What if the interview went badly? What if he didn't hire her?

Red and yellow tulips nodded at her in the light breeze, but she barely noticed. It was Adam's face she saw, in her mind, as she headed down the inn's stone pathway.

From a newspaper clipping attached to the P.I.'s report, she'd learned that Adam had recently left his job at the high school to manage the new community center. The clipping also reported that he was in the process of hiring. It was no coincidence that one of the job openings was for a drama teacher and that she was the perfect candidate. It was fate.

How could he *not* hire her?

A five-minute walk brought her to a large brick-and-glass structure. The complex stood before her like a fortress, daring her to try to infiltrate its walls. Apprehension swept through her. This was a small-town community center? She stood motionless on the front steps, debating whether to turn around. Turn around and run back home. But what kind of life did she have in Hartford? Without Megan it was a life without meaning. Nothing could fill the emptiness that engulfed her. It was like a well that year after year grew deeper and wider.

Hesitating before the tall glass doors, she looked over at the arena adjacent to the main building. The new community center was more than a hub for the arts; it also served as a home for recreational activities as diverse as yoga and ice-skating. Working in the community center would have its perks, she thought, trying to bolster her resolve. Having a rink close to where she worked would be an added bonus. She could skate with Megan. It could be a mother-daughter experience. A bonding activity.

Filled with fresh determination, she walked into the reception area of the main building. Bright and festive watercolors decorated the walls, and one in particular held her attention. Against a backdrop of buildings and street lamps, five children in coats and mittens were gathered in a public square, building a snowman. Spilling its rays onto the snow, the sun created a kaleidoscope of colors, bringing to life the magic of childhood.

"It's wonderful, isn't it?" came a voice from behind her. "It's the work of one of Middlewood's finest artists, Laura Matheson-Logan. Her husband, Jake Logan, built this complex. The painting hung in his office for years before he donated it to the center. He said it was time he shared it with others."

"It's lovely," Rachel said, her gaze locked on the painting. "I've always been envious of artists. They have this amazing ability to capture something illusory and package it into something permanent." She turned around to face the woman. "I do theater work," she said amiably. "Once the play is over, the emotion is gone. All we have left is the memory of how we felt."

"I know what you mean," the woman said. "Nevertheless, I've always admired people who can create living emotion on the fly. The mood may be temporary, but isn't life?" The woman smiled. "I'm Doreen Parker, Administrative Assistant to the Director. Actually, for now I'm the receptionist, secretary and, generally speaking, gopher. We just opened a few days ago when the schools let out, and as you can see—'' she gestured at the crates along the walls ''—we're in the throes of chaos. How can I help you, Miss…?''

"Hartwell. Rachel Hartwell." Even though Rachel had been single for two years, she still went by her married name. *At least my marriage wasn't a total waste,* she thought wryly. *It allowed me to change my identity.* "I have an appointment with Mr. Wessler," she said, quickly filing away the past. If she were to gain her future, she had to concentrate on the present. "I'm here about the drama teacher position."

Doreen appeared to be about sixty, but she was by no means matronly. Her azure linen suit was simple yet chic, her salt-and-pepper hair pulled back into an elegant chignon. Rachel realized that Doreen was appraising her as well, and instinctively knew that nothing could escape the older woman's keen, probing eyes.

"Forgive me for staring," Doreen said. "It's just that you look familiar. I don't know you, do I?"

Rachel's heart skipped a beat. Her mother had grown up in the nearby town of Ridgefield, and had moved to Hartford a month before Rachel was born. What if Doreen had known her? What if, years later, the gossip had made its way back to Middlewood? What if this woman had heard about Beth Cunningham's wild and pregnant daughter?

Once again Rachel was grateful to her ex-husband for giving her his name. "I'm from Hartford," she answered evasively. "A city girl through and through."

"This isn't the city, but I'm sure you'll love it here. Come with me. I'll show you to Adam's office."

Rachel followed Doreen down a long corridor. "Aren't you worried about theft?" she asked, as they headed around a corner. All the windows in the reception area had been left open to dilute the smell of fresh paint. "Isn't there any security?"

Doreen laughed. "You *are* a city girl." Her face grew serious. "I have to admit, Middlewood does have its share of crime. Recently a few neighborhoods were hit with a rash of burglaries. Probably just kids, since all they took were CDs, DVDs, that sort of thing. But to answer your question, we activate an alarm system when the center is closed.... Ah, here we are." She knocked on an unpainted panel door and opened it without waiting for a response.

The room appeared empty. "Damn pole won't stay put," a deep voice growled from inside the closet. "Where is that Farley? He promised he'd have this closet done by noon."

A tall man in a well-tailored but rumpled suit emerged. "Really, Doreen," he reprimanded, "I wish you'd wait for a response before entering."

In the report the investigator had described Adam Wessler as "pompous and fastidious, a man who relishes his privacy." An investigator with a large vocabulary, Rachel had thought, amused. Adam obviously liked his privacy, or he wouldn't have barked at Doreen, and whether or not he was pompous remained to be seen— but fastidious? Standing there grumbling in his wrinkled and dusty suit, he was not what Rachel had expected. True, he was as handsome as in his picture, his nose straight and aquiline, his jaw square and proud, but his untidy appearance caught her by surprise. Holding a hammer in one hand, smoothing his dirt-smudged lapels with the other, he looked more like a gussied-up construction worker than the director of a community center.

There was also the matter of his hair. As in the photo

it was thick and dark, but here in the office smoothness had given way to spiky disarray, as if he'd been running his fingers through his hair in frustration. He turned to place the hammer on his desk, and Rachel had to suppress a smile. In contrast to his gray suit, his tie was brightly colored with a cartoon of the Tasmanian devil. A gift from Megan? In any case, that he chose to wear it contradicted the P.I.'s report, which not only described Adam as pompous and fastidious but also as conventional.

Adam Wessler certainly appeared to be an interesting mix of traits.

He spun around and boldly looked her over. The word *interesting* hardly described him, she realized. All the pictures she had received were in black and white, but she doubted that even a color shot could have conveyed the piercing blaze of his stare. No words or photographs could have prepared her for his steel-blue eyes, which burned into her like a laser.

"Now, Adam," Doreen said as though talking to a child, "Farley said he'd be finished in here by the end of the week. You know the theater takes priority. How can the kids rehearse without a stage? They can't use the cafeteria indefinitely."

"You want priority?" Adam grumbled. "What about this?" He gestured to the wall behind him. The left side was a pleasant shade of green, the right a murky gray.

Doreen clicked her tongue in disapproval. "It's not Farley's fault you changed your mind. What do you think, Rachel? Green or gray?"

Rachel studied Adam as he stood there, his arms folded across his chest, his brow creased with irritation. "They say that green is restful on the eyes," she answered. "It puts the viewer in a calm mood. Like New Age music."

"Who is this woman and why is she talking to me about New Age music?" Even as he spoke to Doreen, Adam's eyes never left Rachel. He rested his gaze on the jacket of her peppermint-green suit and said, "I prefer the gray."

It figures, Rachel thought, trying not to react to his rudeness. "Rachel Hartwell," she said, extending her hand. When he didn't take it, she pulled it back. "I'm here about the opening in the drama department," she continued with forced confidence. She leaned over. "Uh, Mr. Wessler?" Adam had crawled underneath his desk.

"Here it is," he said, emerging triumphantly. "I've been looking for this little gadget." He got off the floor and began fiddling with his computer. "Now maybe I can get e-mail, seeing how my phone will probably never be connected."

"Excuse me for butting in, but I don't see how you can get e-mail without a phone."

"For your information, we have a permanent Internet connection," he said, looking up. "What did you say your name was?"

Rachel had no intention of being turned down for the job simply because her prospective employer was in a bad mood. "Mr. Wessler," she said in a patient voice, "if this isn't a good time for you, I can come back later. At your convenience, of course."

"You see what you've done?" Doreen reprimanded her boss. "It's a wonder you have any staff at all, the way you go on. Why I agreed to work for you in the first place is a mystery."

"It's because you've been secretly in love with me

for years, and you'd run off with me in a heartbeat except that Roger won't let you."

"Just ignore him," Doreen said, dismissing him with a wave. "He always gets delusional when he's irritated. The truth is, my Roger could whip this boy thirty years ago, and he still can today." She laughed when Rachel threw her a confused glance. "My husband and I were friends with Adam's parents," she explained. "These days, I'm kind of a second mother to him."

Doreen seemed like a genuinely warm person, and Rachel felt herself relaxing. "He's lucky to have two mothers," she bantered back. "A man needs all the sound advice he can get."

A silence fell as quickly as a late-summer fog, and Adam's face paled.

What did I say? Rachel thought. She looked at the older woman for guidance, but Doreen's unsmiling face was as sober as Adam's.

"I'll let you two get down to business," Doreen said quietly. Then, just as quickly as it had faded, her smile reappeared, as welcoming as the sun breaking through a cloud. "Good luck, dear. I'm rooting for you."

"I'm sorry about your mother," Rachel said after Doreen had shut the door behind her. "How long has she been gone?"

"My mother is *not* gone. And she's not going anywhere, now or for a long time to come."

"I'm sorry, Mr. Wessler," Rachel apologized again. "I just assumed—"

"Adam," he corrected. "Call me Adam. I, for one, would like to go back to the time when employees addressed their superiors as Mr. or Mrs. Unfortunately those days are gone."

He was pompous, all right. If his ego were any more

bloated, he could run for king. And what was this thing about his mother? Evidently the well-composed Adam Wessler had issues. Issues the P.I. had overlooked. Which was odd, she thought, considering how detailed the P.I. had made his report. Several pages described Megan's life—school, hobbies, friends—right down to her favorite flavor of soda. More pages contained similar information about Adam, although, Rachel conceded, his favorite flavor of soda was more than she wanted or needed to know.

"Ms.," she said curtly.

"Excuse me?"

"The appropriate term is *Ms*. There's no legal basis for an employer to know a prospective employee's marital status." She knew she was treading close to the line—he had the power to make or break her future—but, oh, he was so infuriating!

"*Ms*. Hartwell, let me assure you I don't give a hoot about your marital status. I was merely trying to point out that it is perfectly fine for you to address me by my first name. In fact, it's preferred. One of the center's main goals is to reflect the community, and that includes its values. You know what I mean—apple pie, babies in strollers, Boy Scouts helping elderly women cross the street. One big happy family. It's the kind of Pollyanna image we're trying to promote."

"I take it you don't agree with this philosophy?"

He looked vexed. "It's of no importance whether or not I agree. Now, shall we get started, Ms. Hartwell?"

"Rachel," she corrected. "One big happy family, remember?"

He looked at her sternly for one hard moment, and then an unexpected grin washed across his face, catching her off guard.

She drew in a sharp breath. His whole austere demeanor had vanished, just like that. How could something as simple as a smile, just two lips curling up at the corners, completely transform a face?

And it was such a charming smile. He looked almost boyish, completely unlike the photographs back in her room at the inn.

This time he was the one to extend a hand. "What do you say we start again? I'm Adam Wessler, the arrogant, obnoxious director of this wonderful new establishment."

"Rachel Hartwell," she answered back, returning his handshake. She'd once read that a handshake told a lot about a person's character. His was warm...protective...

She realized she had been holding on too tightly, and feeling the color rise in her face, tore her hand away. "You're not *that* obnoxious," she joked in an attempt to hide her embarrassment.

He let out a hearty roar. "Finally we're agreed on something. Have a seat, Rachel Hartwell, and we'll get down to business. Sorry about the folding chairs. As you can see, not all the furniture has arrived yet." He sat down beside her. "Why don't you start by telling me a little about yourself?"

"You don't have my résumé? I have extras. Here, let me—"

He picked up a sheet of paper from his desk. "I have your résumé. I know what it says. I want you to tell me something I don't know. Something about the kind of person you are. It's not such an unreasonable request."

What could she tell him that wasn't on her résumé? After years of working and studying she'd finally earned her degree, and since then she'd been teaching at a private school in Hartford. Her résumé also described her active involvement in musical and children's theater. Wasn't she what a community-based job required? A well-rounded, *involved* person? What else did he need to know? "I don't understand," she said with trepidation.

No longer smiling, he said, "I'll give you a hint. You can start by telling me why you want to teach here."

"I've always loved kids," she began slowly. "And musical theater. So it was only natural that I would want to pursue a career that involved both." When he didn't respond, she felt her panic rising. What could she say that wouldn't give away her secret? She had to think of something. She had to land this job. And then she remembered the winter scene hanging on the wall in the corridor. The painting wasn't only about the joys of childhood; it was about the joys of small-town living. "There's something else."

"And that is…?"

"I'm tired of the city. I find it too large, too impersonal. I want to live in a small, old-fashioned community. Like you said earlier, apple pie, that sort of thing. You know what I mean, where everyone knows everyone's business." As long as no one finds out mine, she thought.

"You seem to have developed a few notions," he said testily. "It's true that we're a close-knit group, but we're not a bunch of hicks. We nurture the same interest in the arts as do the larger cities, and we don't take well to being patronized."

"You don't understand. I wasn't—"

"Tell me what makes Rachel Hartwell tick."

What was he getting at? What could she say that would persuade him to hire her? Then it dawned on her. He was talking about character. "I sent you a list of references. Didn't you receive it with my résumé?"

None of the people on the list knew anything about her past. Equally important, the school where she taught was closed for the summer. She didn't want anyone there to know she might not be returning. At this point it wouldn't be wise to burn her bridges behind her. Eventually Adam would want to speak to someone regarding her most recent employment, but verification would have to wait until fall. By then, if everything went as planned, it wouldn't matter.

But if her plan failed, she would return to Hartford. She couldn't remain in Middlewood, knowing that Megan was so close yet so out of reach. She couldn't spend the rest of her life looking around every corner, down every street, hoping to catch a glimpse of her daughter, living solely for those moments.

"You still don't get it," Adam said, his gaze boring into her. "I want you to tell me why I should give you this job. Give me one good, concrete reason."

She tried to think of a reply that would please him yet be true to her ideals. "I know what it's like to have a dream," she said finally. "I also know what it's like to have no one to help you nurture that dream. Some children want to be doctors, some firefighters. I wanted to be a skater—but competition was out of the question. Everyone knows how expensive that route is, and now, of course, I'm too old to compete. But if I can make a difference in someone's life, if I can help a child realize his or her dream, then I'll feel as if I've succeeded."

The words she spoke were true. All her life she'd had a need to nurture. When she was small, she'd brought home every stray cat in the neighborhood, and when she was older, she'd gone out of her way to take the side of the underdog. Her mother used to chide her endlessly.

"Lie down with dogs and you'll get up with fleas," she used to say.

"You realize that working here would mean a decrease in salary," Adam said, glancing at her résumé. "This is a community center, not a private school."

"I want to work in a more liberal environment," she said honestly. She wasn't thrilled about taking a cut in pay—paying rent on two apartments would be expensive and the months ahead would be lean—but she was looking forward to working in a more relaxed environment. She was tired of the senseless customs, the strict dress code, the arbitrary rules imposed by the school where she taught. "Besides," she added, "there are benefits. For example, the arena. I still love skating, even though it's no longer my life dream. And it's not as rushed here in Middlewood as it is in the city." This time she was careful not to use the term *old-fashioned*. She wouldn't make that mistake again.

The interview wasn't going as she expected. He was supposed to ask her a few perfunctory questions and get on with it, but the closed look on his face told her he didn't buy what she was saying. Anyone with half a mind could see that she was perfect for the job. What was he getting at?

"Unfortunately, I don't think this is going to work out," he said.

Unfortunately? Was this what it all came down to? All her hopes crushed with one dismissive word? "I don't understand. Won't you just—"

"Do I look like Grace? Puh-leeze!"

A young girl with the brightest red hair Rachel had ever seen had barged into the office. "Will you puh-leeze inform Erika that I have no intention of playing

Grace? What's the matter with that woman? Can't she see I'm meant to be Annie?''

In that moment reality merged with dream, and Rachel wasn't sure if she'd just awakened or fallen asleep. The room around her blurred, and she had to blink to hold back tears that were threatening to steal from her eyes. Tears of joy at seeing her daughter. Tears of joy at hearing her voice.

Adam had asked for one good reason, a concrete reason. There she was, her hands on her hips, scowling in the doorway.

Chapter Two

If it weren't for the hair, she would have sworn she was looking in a mirror, one that reflected what she had looked like at Megan's age. She gripped the edge of her chair. Would anyone else notice?

How could anyone *not* notice?

Doreen had remarked earlier, "You look familiar. I don't know you, do I?"

Rachel dismissed the comment from her mind. It had just been one of those things people said, as benign as "How are you?" or "Have a nice day." How could Doreen—or Adam—know what Rachel had looked like at twelve years old?

"What is it, Megan?" Adam asked in an exasperated voice. "Can't you see I'm in a meeting?"

Rachel tore her gaze from her daughter. From the tense lines on Adam's face she could read the depth of his frustration. It was something, she was sure, that hadn't started just now with Megan's little scene. No, the troubles with his daughter had been going on for some time. Rachel was certain of something else as well, and she breathed a sigh of relief. Adam had not picked up on the resemblance between her and Megan. He looked frustrated, vexed, flustered—everything that seemed to go along with being the single parent of an adolescent girl—yet the likeness that was obvious to Rachel had apparently escaped his notice.

She turned her gaze back to Megan. It was hard to look at her without focusing on the wealth of deep red that curled in ringlets over her forehead and down her neck. Thank God for that hair, Rachel thought. It helped hide the resemblance. Rachel's hair, framing her heart-shaped face and curving under her chin—the shape of face and dainty chin she had bequeathed to her daughter—was a rich brunette, totally unlike Megan's. But even though the pictures the P.I. had sent were in black and white, even without the detailed description he had supplied, Rachel had known that her daughter was a red-head.

She thought back to when she was seventeen, wild and free, holding on to her boyfriend's waist as she snuggled behind him on his motorcycle. She knew she should have worn a helmet—they both should have worn helmets—but wasn't it wonderful riding behind him on his bike, feeling as free as a leaf in the breeze! In those days the word *caution* hadn't been part of her vocabulary. As if it were yesterday, Rachel remembered the way the air had felt blowing on her face as she held on to Colton, watching the wind weave its playful fingers through his long, wavy hair.

Like Megan, his hair had been a deep fiery red.

She remembered the way the nurses had clucked after

Megan was born, swearing they had never seen so much
hair on a newborn. "The devil's crown," one insensitive
nurse had said. "Heiress of sin."

"But Dad, you're always in a meeting!" Megan was
complaining. "Anyway, this concerns business." She
turned her attention to Rachel. "Are you the new drama
teacher? Because if you are, we need to get some things
straight. First of all—"

"Megan!" Adam interrupted sharply. "I'll talk to you
later."

"No, it's all right, Mr. Wes...Adam. I'm interested in
what your daughter has to say."

Two suspicious green eyes—*my* eyes, Rachel
thought—peered at her. "Oh, yeah?" Megan chal-
lenged. "Why?"

"Why?" Rachel repeated, blinking.

"What are you, deaf?"

"Megan!" Adam rose from his chair. "Can't this wait
until later?"

Rachel wanted to laugh. He sounded as if he was
whining. The cool, collected Mr. Wessler was obviously
putty around his daughter, who was, if this outburst was
any indication, sorely lacking in manners. Oh yes, Adam
Wessler needed all the help with Megan he could get.

"It's all right," Rachel assured him. "The question
deserves an answer. And I'm not referring to her question regarding my hearing. You'd be surprised at how
little escapes my ears, or eyes, too, for that matter."

Megan was leaning against the wall, her arms folded
across her chest as though she was a small child demanding a treat. Yet *spoiled* hardly described her, and
Rachel sensed there was more to her attitude than just
bad manners. This child, *her* child, was hurting, and Rachel ached to reach out and hold her.

"It's too bad you have no intention of playing Grace," she said. "She's always been my favorite character in *Annie*. They named her Grace for a reason. And you remind me of her—you're tall and slim, as pretty as a princess—and that's why I'm interested in what you have to say."

"I'm nothing like her!" Megan snapped. "Look at me. Look at this hair." She tugged at a handful of curls as if to make her point. "What's the use in having a father who's running this whole place, if I can't be the star? I can sing and dance every bit as well as that stupid Alice Tucker. Even better. I'm Annie! Why can't anyone see that?"

"I'm envious of you," Rachel said, choosing her words carefully. "I bet you don't need to use any styling aids at all, and what I would give to have that color!"

Megan looked somewhat mollified. "There, you see, Dad? She agrees with me. She thinks I should be Annie."

"I didn't say that," Rachel said, "although I'm sure you'd make a wonderful Annie. It's a shame, though."

"What do you mean?"

"I would have thought that someone as grown-up as you would feel a little silly in the role of Annie. I would have thought that Grace would be your first choice. She's so beautiful and talented, and in the end, we get the idea that she's going to marry the richest, most wonderful man in the world. To me Grace represents the heart in the story. Without her Annie would never have been united with Daddy Warbucks."

"Annie *is* kind of childish," Megan admitted. "Maybe you're right. Maybe I should play Grace. She's much more refined. Worldly, even. It would be more interesting to play someone mature, don't you think?"

"I know it," Rachel said. Worldly? Mature? The way Megan spoke now, you'd think she was eighteen, not twelve. In an instant her entire demeanor had changed from that of a pouting young child to a sophisticated young lady. Girls that age are like that, Rachel thought. One minute they're taking out their old dolls; the next minute they're asking for the keys to the car.

Megan was growing up fast. Too fast. Rachel had missed the first twelve years of her daughter's life, and she was determined not to let another precious minute go by.

"What about my hair?" Megan asked. "I wouldn't have to cut it, would I? What about the color?"

"You won't have to change a thing. You could get a wig from wardrobe. There is a costume department, isn't there?" She addressed her question to Adam.

"Of course there is. What kind of operation do you think I'm running?" His mouth pulled into a tight line. "Actually, there isn't, not really. We're still trying to negotiate deals with costume houses. In the meantime Doreen and Erika make frequent trips to the thrift shops."

"Erika told us we have to bring our own costumes," Megan said. "She told us to ask our mothers to make them." She pulled herself on top of Adam's desk and sat there, kicking her legs. "That was a stupid thing for her to say, don't you think? Considering that at the moment I seem to be fresh out of mothers."

No, you're not, Rachel thought, her heart growing warm. It had taken a little reassuring on her part to convince Megan to take the role of Grace. Like all twelve-year-old girls—like most people—Megan needed to feel important. Wasn't this what mothers did? Instill a sense of self-esteem in their daughters?

"I'm sure Erika didn't mean anything by her comment," Adam said. "And I'm sure that if you asked her, she'd be more than happy to make your costume."

"Let me remind you, she's not my mother."

A warning signal went off in Rachel's head. The P.I.'s report had mentioned that Adam was seeing someone but that it wasn't serious. What if the report wasn't accurate? What if Adam and this woman were keeping their relationship low-key for Megan's sake? It was obvious that Megan disliked her.

"Besides," Megan continued, "that woman wouldn't know the difference between a needle and a haystack."

It was a clever twist to the old adage, and Rachel laughed. "I'm handy with a needle and thread," she volunteered. Hadn't Megan said that the mothers were supposed to make the costumes? "But I wouldn't know my way around a haystack if my life depended on it," she added jokingly.

"Well, there are no haystacks in this center," Adam said, and sat down again.

Even sitting, he was tall. In spite of his disheveled appearance, he had the air of someone used to getting his own way. Rachel studied his face. The photographs she'd received all made him appear hard and unyielding, but seeing him in person, she could tell there was something vulnerable about him. Something a little bit broken. She had an urge to soothe him.

Be careful, she warned herself. You've always been a sucker for a wounded animal. And where did it ever get you? First time around, you were left alone and pregnant. Second time around, you were simply left alone.

"Officially you start tomorrow, but I'd like to meet with you a little later today, say in about an hour, to go over the costume budget. I want you on thrift-shop duty, like the others. Before we meet, see Doreen. She has some forms you'll need to fill out.'' He leaned forward in his chair. ''In the mornings you'll be teaching musical theater, in the afternoons, improvisation. Classes start on Monday, so you'll have today and Monday to get oriented. Erika Johnson is a wonderful drama coach, and she's mapped out all the classes, so you need to meet with her. She's directing *Annie,* which you'll be helping out with as well. You'll have a desk backstage for your paperwork. In the fall your hours will change. Classes and rehearsals will be held after school and in the evenings. Any questions?''

Adam talked so fast, she felt her head spinning. ''I...don't understand. What are you saying?''

Megan shook her head in mock disgust. ''I think she *is* deaf, Dad. Are you sure you know what you're doing?''

He ignored his daughter and flashed his boyish smile at Rachel. ''I'm saying, Ms. Hartwell, that you've got the job.''

''Rachel,'' she said smoothly, trying to conceal her elation. ''Apple pie, remember?''

No matter how much he fiddled with the computer monitor, it wouldn't light up. Dammit, he should be able to figure out this contraption. The problem with technology was that as soon as you got something all figured out, it was already obsolete.

Adam was the first to admit he wasn't too fond of change.

The screen on his desk suddenly came to life. He sat back on his chair. What had just happened? Good question, Wessler. He wasn't referring to the computer; he was thinking about the interview. A stunning young woman waltzes into my office as though she's on some kind of mission, and my brain goes AWOL. How could I have gone against my gut reaction and hired her on the spot?

It had nothing to do with the way she looked. No one could accuse him of that kind of bias. Sure, she was curvy in all the right places, with legs that didn't quit, but he'd hardly noticed. And he'd hardly noticed her face as he'd gone through the motions of conducting the interview. Her skin was smooth and sun kissed, her smile bright and contagious. Her emerald eyes shone with a passion that, these days, was foreign to him—although he hadn't paid much attention to her eyes, either.

No, it was because he needed someone to fill in for the teacher he had originally hired for the position. After deciding she would rather act than teach, Susan Dobbs had suddenly quit and left for New York.

Good luck, he thought. New York was full of would-be actors.

But that wasn't the only reason he had hired Rachel. That wasn't why his brain had turned to oatmeal. It had something to do with his daughter. Only a blind person couldn't have seen the way Megan and Rachel had connected. No sighted person could have missed the way Rachel had glowed like a child on Christmas morning when he'd suggested that Megan show her around the center, or how Megan had eagerly complied.

He knew she was more than qualified for the job. This was children's amateur theater, not Broadway, and she was a teacher with stage experience. But there was something about her, something that didn't add up. Something he couldn't define.

Before Megan had barged in, he had decided to turn

Rachel down, basing his decision purely on instinct. But the skillful way she'd handled the situation with Megan had convinced him to change his mind. When Erika had cast another girl for the part of Annie, Megan had taken the decision as a personal affront—Megan took *everything* Erika did as a personal affront—yet in less than a minute Rachel had persuaded Megan to take the part of Grace. It had been nothing short of amazing. And this was why he had gone against his initial reaction and hired her. Someone with as much understanding of kids as she'd demonstrated was what this place needed. Maybe she was just what Megan needed.

He was always on the lookout for anything that might brighten his daughter's life. She was so temperamental, more so these past two months, ever since his mother had taken a turn for the worse. Recently he'd brought home a puppy from the pound, even though Erika had been against it. "You can't expect someone so troubled to be responsible for another living thing," she'd argued. Erika had been wrong. Cinnamon had quickly become Megan's best friend and confidante, and where the puppy's health and safety were concerned, Megan was like a doting parent. But she was still so moody.

She was high-strung because she was gifted, Erika insisted. Someone with that much talent should be in a special school. The Manhattan School for the Arts had a few openings, but time was running out. Adam had to make a decision soon, to secure a place.

Then there was his mother. He had to make a decision about her, as well.

He stared out the window. Middlewood was a pretty town, with neatly laid-out streets and yards. The downtown streets were lined with antique stores and trendy cafés, and something was always going on—a festival, an exhibit, an organized walk through the hilly grounds. The town was growing fast, and change was something he had trouble with.

The phone rang, taking him by surprise. It's about time that thing worked, he thought, picking up the receiver. But after what he heard on the other end, he found himself wishing that the connection hadn't been fixed. Not that he was ever inaccessible. These days, with one crisis after another at home, he made sure he was never without his cell phone. After a brief conversation he hung up and placed his head in his hands.

He thought back to the past. Except for his years at Berkeley he'd lived in Middlewood all his life. After graduation he married his childhood sweetheart, Cathy, and began teaching at the local high school. Five years later they adopted a baby, and for ten more years they lived a normal, happy life. Then, on the day of their fifteenth anniversary, Cathy had been driving back from the hairdresser's and his world had collapsed.

No, he wasn't very good at handling change. But things *were* changing, and he felt powerless to stop them.

He was about to leave his office, when he remembered his umbrella. The sun shone in through the open window, and the day outside was bright and clear. He was sure the forecast was wrong, but the last thing he wanted was to be caught by surprise as he walked across the parking lot. Like change, surprise was something he didn't handle well.

"Through those doors is the passageway that leads to the arena," Megan said. "Isn't that neat? You don't even have to leave the building."

"Do you skate?" Rachel asked hopefully.

"No, I don't have much time for sports, with acting classes and rehearsals and helping out at home. Dad plays hockey, though. He says it helps him unwind. But I guess that kind of skating is different."

They passed through the main corridor and entered the theater. "This place is wonderful," Rachel said. "I never figured on it being so large!"

"It seats five hundred. Middlewood might be a small town, but we have a reputation for supporting the arts." Megan motioned to the orchestra pit. "We even have our own symphony. They'll be doing the music for *Annie*."

Rachel was touched by Megan's obvious pride in her community. "When do they plan on finishing in here?" she asked as they made their way to the stage. She craned her neck and looked up. A big burly man was standing on the catwalk, hammering.

"Sometime next week. At least that's what Farley says." Balancing herself with one arm, Megan swung onto a crate and sat down. "I suppose I'll have to introduce you to Erika." She rolled the name off her tongue as if it had a sour taste.

"You don't like her, do you?"

"Let me put it this way. If we were putting on *The Wizard of Oz,* she'd be perfect in the role of the witch. I'm just hoping that someone will drop a house on her. Maybe then I won't have to move away."

In her careful scheming Rachel hadn't considered that Adam would ever leave Middlewood. She felt a cold knot form in her chest. "Your father just took on a new job. Why does he want to move?"

"He's not moving, just me," Megan answered. "To some kind of finishing school. Did you ever hear of anything so stupid? A finishing school in this century! Erika calls it an art academy, but she can't fool me. The Manhattan School for the Arts is just a place where East Coast parents can dump their kids.''

"I take it you don't want to go." Rachel's mind was whirling. She supposed she could always apply for a position at the school, but why would they hire her? The Manhattan School for the Arts was world renowned. It wasn't a small private school in Hartford, and it certainly wasn't Middlewood.

Megan shrugged. ''At least I won't be living with Erika. She's been chasing after my father ever since Mom died. Dad says they're just good friends, but if I know Erika, she'll have a ring on his finger before the end of the summer. She wants me out of the picture, except Dad doesn't see it that way. He says she only wants the best for me.''

Rachel had just been reunited with her daughter. She couldn't lose her again. "Have you told your father how you feel?" she asked, hoping she didn't sound desperate.

"What do you think? But he only listens to Erika. He listens to practically everything she tells him, and these days she's telling him that I need a mother. Puh-leeze! Just what I need, a mother who ships her kid off to boarding school. Look, I don't mind if Dad gets married again. It would be kind of cool to have someone around, someone who could help me with my costumes. But not Erika.''

Rachel didn't miss the loneliness in her daughter's voice. "I'd be happy to help you with your costumes," she said softly.

Megan looked at her thoughtfully, then flashed her a bright smile. "I remember. Handy with a needle, clueless about haystacks." She lowered her voice. "Get out that needle, Rachel. You might need it as a weapon.

Here comes the wicked witch of the West.'' She gestured to a slim, petite woman coming up the aisle toward them.

"Get down from there, Megan,'' the woman said, approaching the stage. "What's the matter with you? It's dangerous in here with all this construction. It's like a war zone. Where have you been? Your father's been looking everywhere for you.''

"Hey, don't aim those fake nails at me,'' Megan said, not moving from her perch. "I was only doing what he asked me to do, showing Rachel around. And it's *not* dangerous in here. Farley's way upstage. It's not like he's going to drop a hammer on anyone's head.''

The woman directed her attention to Rachel. "So you're the new teacher,'' she said coolly. "I'm Erika Johnson.''

"Rachel Hartwell. I'm glad to meet you. I understand we'll be working together. And please don't be angry with Megan. She's been so helpful. She's been giving me a tour.''

Rachel made a quick assessment of the woman standing next to her. Erika was poised and sophisticated in a raw silk jacket that closed in a deep vee, and a matching midlength skirt that was slit down the side. Definitely out of place in this dangerous war zone, Rachel thought.

Two gray eyes bored through her. "You must have misunderstood,'' Erika said. "We won't be working together. You'll be reporting to me.'' She turned to face Megan. "Your father had a phone call. There was a minor crisis involving your grandmother, but it's nothing you need to worry about. He had to go home, but he'll be back later to pick you up.''

"Nothing I need to worry about? She's my grandmother!''

"Don't shout at me, Megan. Those were his words, not mine."

"Yeah, right. Hey, Ricky, I've got a great idea. Maybe you can send Grandma away to boarding school, too. Oops, I forgot. They don't ship grandmothers off to boarding schools the way they do kids. They lock them away in homes."

"Watch that mouth of yours," Erika retorted. Then, as though catching herself before she went too far, her voice took on a sugary tone. "That's our Megan for you," she said to Rachel, "always the drama queen. She's one talented little girl."

"Little snot, you mean. Admit it, Ricky, you can't wait to get rid of me."

Erika blew out an exasperated breath. "I refuse to get into this again, especially in front of a stranger. In any case, rehearsal is about to start. They're all waiting for you in the cafeteria."

Megan hopped off the crate. "See what I mean? Even now she's trying to get rid of me. You coming, Rachel?"

"You go on ahead. I have to fill out some papers for Doreen, and then later, when your father returns, I have to meet with him to discuss the costume budget."

Megan set off down the aisle. "If you'll excuse me," Rachel said to Erika, "I'd better get started on that paperwork."

"Just one minute."

What now? Rachel thought.

"I realize that Megan can be a handful, but I don't want you giving her extra attention. For one thing, it wouldn't be fair to the other children, and as a friend of the family, I can tell you that extra attention is precisely what that child doesn't need."

Who did this woman think she was, talking to her this

way? This was the woman who had Adam's undivided attention? This was the woman who presumed to take on the role of Megan's mother? "Is there anything else?"

"Yes, as a matter of fact there is. Let me remind you that Mr. Wessler is a very busy man, so I would appreciate it if you directed all your questions to me. And that includes any questions regarding the budget—although I fail to see how the financial details of this center are any of your concern."

Erika was acting like a jealous shrew. Which was crazy, Rachel thought. Or was it? She hadn't missed the frosty way the other woman had scrutinized her. Although Rachel wanted to tell this impossible woman exactly what she thought of her, she held back. Her sounding off would only get back to Adam, resulting in an invitation to leave. "I see," she said in a controlled voice.

"There's one more thing. Adam is very particular about the image he wants this center to project, and I don't want anything to embarrass him. He mentioned that you were a few minutes late for your interview. The ceremony is at seven-thirty tomorrow evening. Please don't be late."

"Ceremony?" Rachel said, confused. "What ceremony?"

"The center's official opening. Friday night, seven-thirty sharp. Didn't you see the signs on the wall?"

No, but Rachel could see the proverbial handwriting, all too clearly. It was warning her that Erika was someone to be reckoned with. "No, I guess I missed them. But it doesn't make any difference. I won't be going."

"Oh? You have something better to do?"

"I'd like to come, but I don't have...I didn't bring..."

"The attire tomorrow is casual. This is Middlewood, not Hollywood. No one dresses up here. Even that old suit you're wearing would be adequate."

What did she mean by "that old suit"? Who made her the fashion police? "I guess I can dig something up," Rachel said, wanting to tell this woman where she and her attitude could go.

"Good. Now that you and I understand each other, I have a feeling we'll get along just fine."

Oh, we'll get along, Rachel thought. As long as I stay out of your way and you stay out of mine. Except that staying out of each other's way would be impossible now that they would be working together.

Correction. Rachel would be working *for* her. That, Erika had made clear.

Rachel was still angry when she handed the completed paperwork to Doreen.

"You've met Erika," the older woman said, grimacing.

"Is it that obvious?"

"Try not to let her get to you. She likes to think she runs this place, but there's one thing about Adam you should know. At times he might seem like a pushover, but don't let that fool you. No one tells him what to do."

"What are you getting at, Doreen?"

"I'm saying that Erika is all bark and no bite."

Maybe so, Rachel thought as she made her way back to Adam's office, but until she knew exactly what kind of enemy she was dealing with, she would play it safe.

And Erika *was* an enemy. She was making Megan

unhappy, and that alone was enough cause for Rachel to call out the National Guard.

Adam wasn't in his office, and Rachel wasn't sure if she should wait for him or go home. When Erika had told her that all matters concerning the job were to go through her, the message had been clear: stay away from Adam. Yet if Rachel didn't wait for him, Adam might consider her irresponsible. She was in a no-win situation.

She looked at her watch. Good heavens, it was nearly five! The paperwork had taken longer than she'd thought. Well, that decided it. He'd said he wanted to meet in an hour, and an hour had long passed. She headed down the corridor, noting that all the windows had been shut. At the front door she stopped and groaned.

A little rain she could handle, but a person would need more than an umbrella in this weather. She would need a rowboat. Rachel had no choice but to wait it out.

To pass the time, she decided to check out the rink. She went back into the main corridor and found her way to the indoor passageway that led from the center to the arena.

She peered through a small oval window. Inside the arena all the lights were on, and she felt a twinge of disappointment. If she'd known it was open, she would have brought her skates.

Now that would have looked ridiculous, she thought, grinning. Who brought skates to an interview?

She opened the metal door and went inside. What was that noise? *Whish, whish, clunk* sounded over and over, a pattern in her ears. Curious, she walked over to the bleachers and sat down.

On the ice, Adam was swinging a hockey stick as though it were a weapon. He'd changed into sweatpants and a sleeveless jersey. Tied by its arms around his waist, a sweatshirt hung down like a backward apron. He was shooting pucks, one after the other, smashing them against the sideboards. After exhausting his supply of artillery, he would gather it up and start the process over again.

Rachel's nurturing instinct switched on like a light-bulb. Here was a man with a problem. Here was a man in pain.

She watched him steadily, mesmerized by the way he would glide across the ice and then suddenly stop to make his hit. *Whish, whish, clunk.* He wasn't a bad skater, she decided. Her gaze followed him as he moved across the rink. The suit he'd worn earlier had concealed his muscular build, his massive shoulders, his athletic stance. She found herself wondering what it would be like dancing with him on the ice, being lifted into the air by those powerful arms, feeling his hands gripping her waist....

She pushed the thought aside. It was a ludicrous notion. Besides, hockey wasn't figure skating. She doubted if Adam Wessler could adapt to a different set of rules—even if it was just about skating. He was a stickler, all right. She couldn't believe he had hired her after she'd had the audacity to show up late for her interview! My, my, a full minute late—the minute she had spent outside the tall glass doors of the center, deliberating whether to turn around and run. It also irked her that he had mentioned her tardiness to Erika. The two of them deserved each other, with their picky ways.

Erika, picky? Another word came to mind, but Rachel was loath to repeat it. Just what was that woman's problem? Erika had acted as though she considered Rachel a personal threat. As if Rachel could be interested in a man so...fastidious. Not in this lifetime, no matter how many scars he had.

Erika had it all wrong. *She* was the threat, not Rachel. As far as Rachel was concerned, anyone who even looked the wrong way at Megan was a threat, and Erika had done more than her share of glowering.

If Rachel honestly believed that Erika cared for Megan, she would back off, as painful as that would be. She would pack her bags and head back to Hartford. All she really wanted was to make sure her child had a mother watching over her, someone who had Megan's best interest at heart. Adam was Megan's legal father, and he had a right to choose whomever he wanted as his wife.

Unless his choice was wrong. Unless the woman he chose was planning to stash his daughter—Rachel's daughter—away in some boarding school.

"No one tells him what to do," Doreen had said.

Maybe no one could tell him what to do, but Erika was talking and he seemed to be listening. Maybe Adam and Erika deserved each other, but there was no way Rachel would allow that woman to have a say in Megan's life.

As though sensing her presence, Adam looked up. She smiled and waved.

Chapter Three

Left foot over right, right foot over left. With a series of quick, forward crossovers, Adam stroked across the rink to the bleachers. He brought his feet together, bent his knees and swiveled to an abrupt stop. "Well, well, it's Ms. Hart-*well*," he said teasingly, passing through the gate. "Here to watch me skate?"

Not only was he pompous, he was downright presumptuous. "I didn't know you were here when I came. And I wouldn't describe what you were doing out there as skating. More like war maneuvers."

He sat down next to her and pulled off his gloves. "If you didn't come to see the heroic hockey hotshot in action, what brings you to the arena?"

"We were supposed to meet, but you weren't in your office. I'm just passing time, waiting for the storm to let up before I go back to the inn."

He tapped himself on the forehead. "The meeting. We

were going to talk about the costume budget. Sorry about that. I had a family emergency earlier, and the meeting slipped my mind."

Just like that, he abandoned his flamboyant facade, and her annoyance dissolved. "Is everything all right?" she asked, concerned.

He shrugged. "Just another episode in the continuing saga of the Wessler household. We'll get over it."

A strand of hair had fallen down his forehead, and she resisted the urge to smooth it away. "You should wear a helmet."

He smiled with faint amusement. "Do *you* wear a helmet when you skate?"

He didn't fool her with that lofty grin; his shell was just a veneer. "No, but I don't have pucks getting shot at me from left and right." She motioned to his jersey. "You should wear long sleeves. What if you fell? You'd make mincemeat of your skin."

"The ice wouldn't dare meet my face, and in case you didn't notice, I've been doing all the shooting in this one-sided war."

One-sided war? A revealing choice of words for someone who was supposed to be so private. He might not be as open as a clam in a cookout, but he was definitely loosening up. This was going to be easier than she'd thought. A man's confidence was easy to win when he wasn't wearing his armor.

And win his confidence was what she aimed to do. She and Adam were going to become friends. Good friends. It wasn't enough for her to become part of Megan's life; she had to embed herself in his, as well. How else could she persuade him that sending Megan away was no solution? How else could she get him to see that Erika wasn't the kind of role model Megan needed?

"If it's one-sided, who are you fighting?" she prompted.

"Why don't you tell me? You seem to be full of advice."

Might as well dive right in, she thought. They weren't bosom buddies yet, but this was as good a time as any. "You're fighting yourself. And you're in a deadlock."

"Do tell. Go on."

"I don't think it was the incident at home that started this particular war. It's part of the reason, but I have a feeling there's a lot more going on."

"And I have a feeling you're going to tell me exactly what that is."

Got that right, Rachel thought. He asked, didn't he? "I think you're undecided about Megan going away to school."

"My daughter's been blabbing again. What else did she say?"

"Please don't be angry with her. She just needed someone to talk to. Can't you tell she's upset?"

"She can talk to whomever she pleases," he answered tightly, "but for your information, I'm fully aware of how my daughter feels. And, I might add, I'm not undecided."

Rachel's heart sank. "So it's definite? You're sending her away?"

"I'm not sure I like the way you said that. I'm not sending her away, I'm furthering her education." He stared out onto the ice. "Ah, hell, it's not just her education I'm thinking of. I guess you've already figured that out, too. Megan has problems, like that mouth of hers. She's defiant and rebellious, and I'm convinced she sneaks out of the house every chance she gets. But no matter how much I threaten her, she denies it, and she won't tell me who she hangs out with. Frankly, the whole thing scares me.''

Rachel remembered the scene in his office. She'd thought that Megan was a little ill-mannered, but that it wasn't serious. Nothing the guidance of a loving mother wouldn't fix. So far she hadn't seen anything to warrant what Adam had told her, but she knew how deceptive appearances could be.

She recalled her dreams, and a wave of anxiety swept through her. Two years ago a voice had begun to call out to her, soft and wistful, while she slept. With a certainty she couldn't explain, Rachel knew that something had happened. Worried that her daughter was in some kind of trouble, she contacted the adoption agency, but her request for information was denied. The records were to remain sealed.

Then, two months ago the dreams changed. The voice in the night was no longer faint and distant, but insistent and compelling, demanding to be heard. Determined to find her daughter, Rachel had hired a private investigator. She'd learned that two years ago—when the dreams first started—Megan's adoptive mother had been killed in a car crash. But the P.I. hadn't mentioned another crisis. Why had the dreams changed? The question wasn't something she could ask Adam. Not only would she rouse his suspicions, he would think she was crazy.

''You think sending her away will solve her problems,'' she stated, trying to keep her voice steady. ''Do you really think this is what she needs?''

''What she needs is a fresh start.''

A fresh start? It was Erika who wanted a fresh start—without his daughter. Rachel wanted to jump up and shake some sense into him. ''Megan is feeling insecure. All girls her age go through it, but it's worse for her, not having a mother. And now you're asking her to leave her home, the only home she's ever known. You grew up here—surely you can understand how difficult the thought of leaving must be. I know *I* couldn't do it.''

''How did you know I grew up here?''

''Excuse me?''

''You heard me. How did you know?''

''The way Megan talked about Middlewood, I, uh, just figured that you were a born-and-bred native.''

He looked at her through narrowed eyes. ''I'm mystified. You said, 'I know I couldn't do it.' Didn't you just move here from Hartford?''

If she continued to blurt things out, she'd blow her cover in no time. She had to be more careful, but it wouldn't be easy. Adam had a way of looking at her that was sharp and knowing. Even if she never said a word, she was afraid his probing steel-blue eyes would uncover her secret.

''Leaving Hartford didn't bother me. All I meant was that if I'd had a real home, I never could have left it.'' Even when he looked at her through half-closed eyes, the way he was looking at her now, it was as if he was seeing right through her.

When he didn't speak, she felt she had to offer more of an explanation. ''My mother is a concert pianist,'' she said cautiously. ''She moved up quickly in the music world, and we moved around a lot. Even though I ended up in Hartford, I learned not to become attached to any one place.''

His eyes softened, surprising her. ''Sorry. I didn't mean to give you the third degree.''

She almost sighed aloud with relief. She was off the hot seat. ''What about Megan?'' she asked, glad to turn the conversation away from the past. "You must have other reasons for wanting to send her away to school."

"You've met Erika, haven't you? I don't know what Megan told you, but Erika is more than just the head of the drama department, such as it is. She and I have been friends for a long time now, and we—" He shifted uneasily on the bench. "I didn't mean to bore you. I don't know why I'm telling you all this."

Rachel knew exactly why. The poor guy didn't have a chance. When it came to wounded animals, she was the local veterinarian. She'd always been a magnet for the wounded, and from the way Adam had been beating up the sideboards, she could tell he was as wounded as they got. "You're not boring me. I like Megan, and I'd like to help."

He hesitated before continuing. "Megan is a talented young actress. Erika believes she has a future on the stage. She thinks that the Manhattan School for the Arts will provide her with the tools she'll need to succeed, and I think she might be right."

Might be right? Maybe he was undecided after all, she thought with hope. "And on the other hand?"

"What other hand?"

"So far you've given me reasons why Megan should go to this school. What are the reasons for her staying?"

He leaned forward, resting his elbows on his knees. "There's plenty of time for Megan to think about her future. If one day she wants to go to New York, I won't stand in her way. But she's still so young. In the meantime, what's wrong with community theater? With me working here, we'll get to spend time together. Although…"

"Although what?" Rachel asked when he didn't continue.

"I'm not sure about the play, *Annie*. It's no secret that Megan was adopted, and now that Cathy is…gone, what if she gets it in her head to go looking for her biological mother, like Annie?"

Rachel's heart was thudding so loudly, she was sure Adam could hear. She didn't want to discuss Megan's adoption. "*Annie* is a wonderful play," she said a little too loudly, as if to drown out the pounding in her chest. "Kids love it. The music is great, the scenery is imaginative, and it ends on such a happy note."

"I'm not questioning its entertainment value, I'm worried about Megan opening up Pandora's box. But it's not just that. I'm also questioning the negative values the play projects. For one thing, Annie gets everything she wants while the rest of the world goes on starving."

"It's just a story," Rachel said. "Escapism. Entertainment. Who wouldn't want to be rich? And you forget that Annie finds love and acceptance. To me, this is emphasized much more than the material aspect. The play doesn't project negative values at all! How can you possibly think that?"

"Whoa," he said, holding out his hand as if to ward her off. "Take it easy. It's not worth starting a war over. You said it yourself, it's just a story. And you can ignore what I said about Pandora's box. It was just a thought. A crazy, paranoid thought. Megan would never go searching for her natural mother. Cathy was the only mother she ever knew, and they were close. Closer than most mothers and daughters."

"You're right," Rachel said in a small voice. "It's just a story." But it wasn't just a story. It was her life.

An uncomfortable silence ensued. "It's back to the ice," he said after clearing his throat self-consciously. "Let's meet in the morning to discuss costumes."

She rose from the bench. "I should be going. The rain has probably let up by now."

"Don't bet on it. It's not supposed to clear until later tonight. After I'm done here, I'll give you a lift."

"You don't have to drive me. I can get a taxi."

He laughed. "You'd have a better chance at winning the lottery than getting a taxi. Middlewood is a great town, but transportation isn't one of its best features. School buses and a two-car taxi stand just about does it. And even if you're lucky enough to get one of the cabs to come, it'll take at least an hour, most likely two." He ran his fingers across her hand. "Forget about walking. You're like an icicle. Can't have my new drama teacher getting pneumonia."

As if on cue, she sneezed.

"Here, take this," he said, untying the sleeves of his sweatshirt from around his waist. "If you're going to stay and watch me mutilate the boards, you'll need to cover up. I've been working up a sweat, but for you it must be like winter in here."

"No, I couldn't—"

"Don't be stubborn," he said, handing her the sweatshirt. "You must be freezing in that thin suit. And it's a nice suit, by the way. I know I acted like a jerk back there in my office, the way I criticized your outfit, and I apologize. Actually, I've always liked that shade of green."

"You didn't criticize—"

"I don't even like gray," he said, interrupting her again, his eyes crinkling with gaiety. "I must have been on a mental vacation when I asked Farley to paint the walls that dingy tone."

There was something gentle and contagious about his

humor. He was thoughtful and considerate, and for Megan's sake she was glad.

She pulled the shirt over her head, catching a whiff of the scent lingering in the material. It was a masculine scent, reminding her of oak and earth.

She warmed up immediately. It was as if the heat had radiated from his body, right through the fleece and into her blood. A delicious shudder moved down her spine.

It had nothing to do with his cocky, boyish smile. It had nothing to do with his strong, athletic body or the way he'd slammed those pucks against the wall like a man with a purpose. And it had nothing to do with the way she had tingled when he'd brushed his fingers across her hand. No, it had nothing to do with any of that.

As she watched Adam skate away, a voice popped into her head. At first she thought it was Megan's, but then realized it was her own.

Puh-leeze!

"She won't start," Adam muttered, fiddling with the key in the ignition. "I think it's the switch."

"Why don't you just buy a new car?" Megan piped up from the back seat. "What's the use in having money if you don't spend it?"

Over his shoulder Adam cast her a stony look. He wasn't about to discuss his financial situation with his daughter, especially with Rachel sitting next to him in the car. "Ethel has a few miles left in her yet," he said, although he doubted the truth in these words. If this relic didn't have major surgery soon, it would probably disintegrate before his eyes.

He knew what Erika would have said to his reply. She would have accused him, once again, of not wanting to let go. Maybe she was right. The '59 Chrysler DeSoto was more trouble than it was worth. It was always in the shop, and parts were hard to find, but it had been the last Christmas gift from his wife. It had been an extravagance, but Cathy had known how much he loved these old classics. They decided to trade in both their cars and buy a sport utility vehicle. Cathy would use the SUV and he would zip around in the DeSoto.

If it hadn't been so tragic, it would have been ironic. She'd had second thoughts about giving him the DeSoto—it doesn't look safe, she'd said. And yet it had been *her* car, a brand-new SUV that was supposed to absorb the shock of impact, that had folded like an accordion when the other driver had run the light.

"Did you ever hear of anything so ridiculous?" Megan said. "He actually named this old heap."

"Ethel was my great-aunt," Adam explained to Rachel. He turned the key again and this time Ethel purred. "My mother's aunt. The story goes that she had a great—" He glanced at his daughter in the rearview mirror. "Let's just say that this car was made to last."

"Could've fooled me," Megan quipped.

"In that case I'm grateful to both Ethel *and* her owner," Rachel said. "The next time the forecast says rain, I'll believe it. I appreciate the lift, Adam."

"My pleasure," he said and meant it, but for the life of him, he didn't know why he felt that way. Rachel was one nosy woman. Tricky, too. Look how fast she'd managed to get him to reveal his feelings about *Annie*. He groaned inwardly. After the preachy things he'd said, she must think he was a moron.

"The inn isn't far from here, but I would have drowned in this storm," she said, looking out the window.

He shifted into gear and pulled out of the lot. "When do you plan on looking for an apartment?"

"I thought I'd scout around this weekend. As charming as it is, I can't live at the inn indefinitely."

"If you want charming, I know of an apartment you can sublet. The tenant is a friend of mine. He's away on a one-year sabbatical in France, and the landlord is willing to sublet on a month-to-month basis. Why not take a look at it? Living there temporarily would give you time to get to know the different neighborhoods before making a commitment to any one place."

"Is it furnished?"

"Yes. Is that a problem? Of course it's a problem. You'll want to have your own things with you."

"No, actually I would prefer it furnished." She opened her purse and took out a pad and pen. "What's the landlord's number? I'll give him a call when I get back to the inn. I'd like to see the place tonight, if I can."

Adam rattled off the number. He wanted to know what she was planning to do with her own furniture, but he kept silent. Unlike some people, *he* wasn't nosy.

As if she could read his mind, she said, "Since I won't be staying in the apartment permanently, it would be silly to move all my things twice, don't you think? For now, I'll just leave my things, uh, stored where they are."

"Rachel, why don't you come over for dinner?" Megan asked. "The apartment is practically around the corner. Dad could drive you over there after we eat."

Adam caught a glimpse of Rachel's face. She was looking at him expectantly. He didn't want her to get the wrong idea, especially after the way he had confided in her at the arena. Sure, she was attractive, and he couldn't help but notice the concern in her eyes when they had talked about Megan, or the way her cheeks had flushed when he'd complimented her suit, or the way she'd crossed and uncrossed her legs when something seemed to bother her. But his life had enough complications and he sure as hell didn't need another one. "I'm sure Rachel already has plans."

"Puh-leeze! What plans could she have? It's not as if she knows anyone in this town. And Paula is making chicken potpies. Paula takes care of us," Megan explained to Rachel. "I bet her food is a lot better than the food at the inn. Don't eat there, Rachel. What if you get food poisoning? Who'll replace you at the center?"

Rachel laughed. "Actually, I've heard that the food there is pretty good. But your father is right. I have plans. I already made reservations."

Adam pulled into the circular driveway outside the inn, and Megan made one last stab. "Won't you change your mind, Rachel? I want you to meet Cinnamon. She's my very best friend in the world, even though she's a messy eater."

"Sorry, Megan. I'll have to meet your friend another time."

"Cinnamon is her dog," Adam said. "I think our Grace Farrel has an ulterior motive. She probably wants your opinion about Cinnamon playing Sandy, the mutt that befriends Annie and follows her everywhere. I, for one, think it's a terrible idea. Cinnamon may be sweet, but she's as dumb as a box of rocks. Completely untrainable. What if, during the performance, she gets it in her head to do her business?"

Megan looked mortified. "Cinny would never do that!"

"And isn't Sandy supposed to be male?" Adam pressed on. "As in, 'Here, boy!'"

"Dramatic license," Megan said. "We can make our own rules."

"You mean poetic license," Rachel said, laughing, "but you have the right idea."

"She's not even the right color," Adam persisted. "Shouldn't she be bright orange?"

"That's the comic strip," Megan said. "It's supposed to be wacky. This is a play. More like real life."

Rachel glanced at Adam. "We wouldn't have to change a thing."

"You see, Dad? Rachel thinks that Cinny should be Sandy."

The way those two connected, you'd think they'd known each other forever. Adam felt like a heel. He knew that Rachel had declined Megan's invitation to dinner only because he hadn't backed it up. An idea occurred to him. "Why don't you stop by for coffee after you've seen the apartment? Paula makes a mean batch of brownies." What was the harm in one cup of coffee? Coffee wasn't dinner. Besides, he was doing it for Megan.

"Say you'll come," Megan said excitedly. "Please, Rachel? I could show you my scrapbook. It's got clippings of every performance I've been in. My mother started it when I was four years old, and Dad's been keeping it going."

"I'd love to see your scrapbook," Rachel said. "And I'd love to meet Cinnamon."

Looking at Rachel's bright smile, Adam began to doubt the wisdom of his invitation. What if she *were* entertaining ideas about him? He didn't want to lead her on. He liked his life the way it was. After Cathy died, it had taken a while, but he'd finally managed to pull himself together. There were still times he found it hard to get up in the morning, to go about his day as if his heart hadn't been ripped from his chest, but for the most part, he was fine. Content. He had Megan, he had his mother, he had his job. And then there was Erika.

Erika was a good sport. He knew how much she had sacrificed. When the council had offered him this position, she'd given up her administrator's job at the musical theater in Ridgefield to work for him at the center. He also knew how difficult for her these past two years had been, helping out with his family. He owed her so much.

He waited until Rachel had disappeared into the inn before he drove off. The rain was coming down harder now, and even though he'd switched the wipers to max, the windshield remained foggy and he couldn't see clearly.

Rachel followed the landlord up the two flights of stairs. "This house is over a hundred years old," he said. "It was split into six apartments and remodeled about ten years ago by Logan Construction."

"The firm that built the community center," Rachel said.

The small landing featured an octagonal etched-glass window high in the wall. The landlord nodded toward one of two white doors. "Your neighbor is in Alaska for the summer, so it'll be plenty quiet." He opened the other door and reached inside to flick on a light switch, then stood back for Rachel to enter.

Simply furnished with a daybed, bureau, dinette set and bookcase, the apartment was tiny, but the exposed roof beams that soared overhead created an illusion of spaciousness. The ceiling, walls and wide wooden floor-boards were painted creamy white, and light from the track fixtures spilled across the satiny surfaces. Rachel walked across the room toward a pair of French doors leading out to a small balcony.

"Lots of light during the day," the landlord said. "Pretty garden in the yard." He opened two doors near the entrance. "Closet and bathroom here, and over there—" he motioned across the counter "—the Pullman kitchen."

Everything was small in scale, yet efficiently planned. A range and half-size fridge were set into the wall, tucked next to the cabinetry. The closet was fitted with wire baskets, racks and shelves. Rachel walked into the small blue-and-white-tiled bathroom, where there was even a claw-footed tub. A stacked washer and dryer were next to the sink.

She rejoined the landlord. "I'll take it."

On the short drive to Adam's house she marveled at her luck. The apartment was welcoming and airy, and it was furnished. Although the rent was higher than she'd planned on, it was within her budget. But most important, even though the apartment was three miles from the community center, it was just a hop and a skip from Adam's house. A hop and a skip from Megan.

Rachel was smiling as she rang the bell. She heard a dog barking inside the house, over the din of a TV. "Will someone turn off that idiot machine?" Adam shouted. "And someone get the door!"

"I'll get the door!" Megan called back. "And you'd better be talking about the TV, not Cinny. She's not an idiot!" She swung the door open and beamed at Rachel. Behind her, a chestnut-brown cocker spaniel was running back and forth, yapping noisily.

Adam came into the foyer. "Rachel, hi. Sorry about the mayhem. Come on in. How did you like the apartment?"

"It's wonderful! In fact—"

"I'll get my scrapbook," Megan said, and ran down the hallway toward the narrow staircase, which in traditional Colonial style divided the house in two.

"Who turned off the TV? Did I tell anyone to turn off the TV?" A woman about Doreen's age appeared in the foyer, wearing an old bathrobe and floppy slippers. "Where's that old bat?" she grumbled. "I have a good mind to fire her. Paula!"

Adam took the woman's hands in his. "Mom, this is Rachel Hartwell. She's going to be teaching at the center. Rachel, this is my mother, Evelyn Wessler."

Evelyn Wessler bore a strong resemblance to her son. Her eyes were the same piercing blue, her cheekbones high and angled. She carried herself with the same pride, but Rachel was convinced that this was more the result of environment than heredity. Megan held that same pride.

Another older woman was just a step behind Evelyn. Her eyes were gentle and understanding, her smile warm. "It's time for your medication," she said to Evelyn, "and then it's off to bed."

"Paula, this is Rachel Hartwell," Adam said. "Rachel, Paula Hutchison. Paula helps take care of us."

"You mean *me,* don't you?" Evelyn corrected. "Paula helps take care of *me.* For some reason my son seems to think I need looking after. I tell you, it's humiliating."

"It's difficult being a single parent," Rachel said tactfully. "He's lucky to have both you and Paula to help out."

Evelyn peered at her closely. "Are you saying I can't take care of Megan?"

"Not at all. I just know how much of a handful a girl Megan's age can be. You're still the one in charge, I can tell."

"You got that right. Smart girl, this one. What's her name, Adam?"

He frowned. "It's Rachel, Mom. I already told you. Rachel Hartwell."

"Well, it's true I can always use the extra help," Evelyn said. "Maybe it's a good thing Paula lives here, even if she is a nuisance. For one thing, I need to replace the curtains. Did you ever see anything so ugly? Maybe we shouldn't fire the old bat, after all. Who else is going to watch Megan while I'm fixing up the house? Who else is going to bathe her and feed her?"

"I told you, Mom, the curtains are fine. Now why don't you let Paula help you upstairs? You have to take your pills."

"I don't need any pills, for pity's sake. I'm not sick, I'm just old."

Rachel felt a stitch in her heart. Evelyn Wessler wasn't old. She appeared to be in her early sixties, around the same age as Doreen and Paula.

"It's just a mild painkiller. You know you won't be able to sleep without it." Adam gently steered her toward the staircase. "Two months ago she fractured her wrist," he explained to Rachel. "It hasn't been the same since."

Evelyn whirled around. "Don't do that! Don't talk about me as if I'm not here. You'll have plenty of opportunity for that soon enough, after that hussy who's been chasing after you sends me away. Oh, I know she can't wait. She's counting the days."

"Now, Evelyn, you don't mean that," Paula said, taking her arm. "Come on, let's get you ready for bed. Say good-night to the company."

"Do you hear the way they talk to me? Like I'm a child. I can get into bed by myself, thank you very much." She shrugged away Paula's arm. "It was nice to see you again, Beth. Maybe next week we can have lunch."

Beth. Rachel felt as if she'd been punched in the stomach. Her mother's name was Beth. Had Evelyn known her? In her confusion, was she mistaking Rachel for Beth?

"Her name is Rachel, Mom." Adam gave his mother a warm hug and waited for her to disappear with Paula up the staircase before he spoke again. "Sooner or later she'll get it straight," he said, smiling at Rachel apologetically. "Let's have that coffee."

In the kitchen he poured them each a cup, his hand shaking visibly. How long had Evelyn been like this? Rachel wondered. She wanted to reach out and cover his hand with hers, but she held back, afraid of embarrassing him with such a display of empathy. But it wasn't her reticence that stopped her. Still disturbed by what Evelyn had called her, she felt her hands shaking as much as his.

"It's been especially hard on Megan, watching her grandmother deteriorate," he said. "The disease is taking its toll on everyone."

Rachel had known about his mother's condition from the P.I.'s report, but she wasn't about to blurt out something she couldn't otherwise have known. That was a mistake she didn't want to repeat. "Are you talking about Alzheimer's? Isn't she too young?"

"Early-onset Alzheimer's can manifest symptoms in the late forties and early fifties," he explained grimly.

She looked at his sad, defeated face. Once again, she wanted to reach for him. From the way he had talked to his mother, from the way he had taken his mother's hands and hugged her, she could see he was a kind man, a compassionate man.

Maybe I can tell him who I am, she thought. Maybe he'll be receptive to my situation. Two years ago, when she'd tried to arrange a meeting through a mediator, she'd been told that the adoptive father—whose identity was not revealed—wanted nothing to do with her. Maybe he had changed. Maybe now he'd relent.

She decided she would tell him who she was, before the evening ended. So much for her plan to sway Adam and Megan over the course of the summer. Oh, she still wanted Erika out of the picture. The woman was causing Megan pain, and that was something Rachel wouldn't stand for—that and boarding school.

Cinnamon skittered into the kitchen and began licking Rachel's shoes. Megan was close behind, carrying a pink-gingham-covered album. "Cinny, stop that!" she reprimanded, dropping the album onto the table. "You're blowing the audition!"

Rachel laughed and tickled the spaniel behind her ears. "She sure is friendly. I think she'd be adorable as Sandy."

Megan's face lit up. "Really? Erika hates the idea. She calls her a flea nest. What does she think will happen? A swarm of insects is going to storm the auditorium and take over the place? Cinny does *not* have fleas."

"You'd have to train her to come to Alice Tucker, the girl who's playing Annie," Adam said. "And not all the scenes have Sandy in them. What would you do with Cinny then?"

"She likes Rachel. She'll stay with her backstage. I bet if Rachel calls her, she'll come. Go on, Rachel, go to the window and call her."

"This I have to see," Adam said. "That dog wouldn't cross the room if a steak dinner called out to her."

Rachel gently nudged away the spaniel and stood up. "Now stay till I call you," she said firmly. The dog cocked her head and looked up with alert brown eyes.

"See? She's not moving. She listens to you! Now call her, Rachel," Megan said after Rachel had moved across the room. "See if she'll come."

"Come here, Cinny," Rachel beckoned. "Come here, girl!"

In an instant Cinnamon was at Rachel's feet, licking her shoes.

"I told you, Dad. Cinny likes her! You'll see, she'll listen to Rachel offstage. So can she be Sandy? Please?"

"Oh, all right," he said with resignation. "We'll give it a try. But she can only come to rehearsal when she's in a scene, and if she acts ups, we'll have to replace her."

"What kind of understudy could we get for a dog?" Megan asked, rolling her eyes. "A goldfish?"

Rachel laughed again. She sat back down and reached across the table. "Is this the scrapbook? Let's take a look."

They went through Megan's scrapbook, and with each page Rachel felt her heart constrict. There was Megan at four, adorable in a frilly pink tutu, at her first ballet recital. There was Megan, age six, dressed as a rabbit in an Easter pageant. There was Megan, age ten, playing Wendy in *Peter Pan*....

After the last page had been turned, the last memory shared, Rachel rose from her chair. "It's getting late," she said, her throat aching with remorse for the years she had forfeited. "I should get back to the inn. I want to settle up tonight so I can move into the apartment first thing in the morning, before heading to the center."

"I'll walk you to your car," Adam said. "Megan, why don't you scoot upstairs and see how your grandmother is doing?"

Megan looked at her father and then back to Rachel. "Sure, Dad," she said, grinning from ear to ear. "Take your time."

So Megan likes to play matchmaker, Rachel thought with amusement. She wasn't surprised. At the arena Adam had said that he and Erika were friends, but according to Megan and Evelyn, Erika had other ideas. There was no way Megan would ever accept Erika as a stepmother, and was probably looking for potential replacements. But for Rachel a romantic entanglement was out of the question. It was all fantasy, anyway. Mere illusion. It clouded your judgment and caused you to make mistakes. And it always led to heartache.

She followed Adam outside, into the damp air. The rain had dwindled to a drizzle, and moisture was rising from the sidewalk in a cloud of mist. She drew in a breath. "There's something you should know," she began, her pulse beating an erratic rhythm.

"You don't have to say it," he said, chuckling. "Megan is always trying to set me up. Her teachers, a divorced mother of a friend, the widow who owns the bookstore... She has it in her head that I'm unhappy. With my schedule, who has time to date? I keep telling her that I'm not in the market for a wife, but Megan keeps trying and the women keep calling."

The man was as conceited as a rooster in a henhouse. Did he actually think she was out to snare him? "Don't worry," she said tersely. "I'm not in the market for a husband."

"I didn't mean to imply you were." He smiled at her in his boyish way, making her regret she had snapped at him. "Here we are again," he said, "back on the wrong foot. Look, I want you to know that I'm glad you and Megan are becoming friends. For some reason she relates to you, and I think you'll be a good influence. That crowd she hangs out with…I'm terrified that one day…that she'll…"

"Nothing is going to happen to her," Rachel assured him. She wouldn't allow it.

"You don't understand," he said, pain registering in his eyes. "I lost my wife because of a drunk driver. They say that the crash happened so quickly, she couldn't have seen it coming. I'll grow a third eye if I have to, to keep a close watch, but I swear on my life, I won't let anything or anyone take Megan away from me."

What could she have been thinking? There was no way she could reveal her identity at this time. Adam would consider her an adversary, someone who was plotting to take away his daughter. She had no reason to believe that in the past two years, ever since he had denied the request to meet with a mediator, he had changed his mind. If the situation had been reversed, if she were the adoptive parent and Adam wanted to establish ties with his child, wouldn't she think of him as a threat?

She had to stick to the original plan. She would wait until her life was intertwined with Megan's, making it impossible for Adam to turn her away. She knew that what she was planning wasn't exactly straightforward, but was it really so wrong? Was it wrong to reach out for your child? Was it wrong to want something so badly you almost believed you could hope it into being? She didn't want to take Megan away from him. All she wanted was to be there for her daughter, to shower her with a mother's love.

She unlocked the door to her car. So much for openness, she thought, dismayed. But it wasn't just guilt that assailed her. For the first time since she'd concocted the plan, she felt like a fraud.

Chapter Four

"I see you made it on time," Erika said, meeting her in the corridor. "Of course, the inn is just a block away. It would have been inexcusable for you to be late."

How did Erika know she'd been staying at the inn? Rachel realized that she'd have to watch what she said to anyone; somehow everything she mentioned got back to this woman. Knowledge was power, and the less Erika knew, the better.

"She's not staying there anymore. She's renting Uncle Steve's apartment."

"Megan!" Rachel sang out happily. "What are you doing here so early?"

"I always come with Dad in the morning. He lets me help Doreen. You know, filing and things like that. He even pays me," she said, her face shining with pride.

"You shouldn't sneak up on people," Erika repri-manded. "And let me remind you that Steven Parker is not your uncle. I don't know why you insist on calling him that."

"Just because he's not my father's real brother, doesn't mean I can't call him uncle. Just because you don't like him, doesn't mean I have to stop."

Ignoring Megan's comments, Erika turned her attention to Rachel. "I didn't realize that Steve had put an ad in the paper."

"He didn't. Adam told me about the apartment."

"On the way home," Megan added. "We gave her a lift. And later she came over for coffee. Cinny positively adored her! Dad said that Cinny could play Sandy."

"Really," Erika said. "I would think, Megan, that you would have better things to do than parade that dog of yours in front of strangers. Like studying your lines. You're already way behind the others. That reminds me, have you started on your costume?"

"Rachel said she'd help me. We're going to work on it this weekend."

Rachel hadn't said any such thing, but she was more than happy to take advantage of her daughter's little white lie. Silently she thanked Erika. Because of her, Rachel would be spending Saturday with her daughter.

"I'd better find Doreen," Megan said. "It's time to go to work."

Her face was so solemn, Rachel had to suppress a smile. Whatever problems her daughter might have, they had nothing to do with her not taking responsibility seriously. "What time do you eat?" she asked. "Would you like to meet for lunch?"

"Great idea! I can show you how to kick the machine to get a free soda." Megan waved and set off down the corridor. When Rachel turned to follow, she was arrested by the chill in Erika's voice.

"Just one moment."

Here we go again. "Yes?"

"I thought I told you not to give that girl extra attention."

"I'm just helping out. She doesn't have—"

"You've already got the job. You can drop the Suzy Sunshine act. I don't know what kind of game you think you're playing, but if you want to continue working here, I suggest you end it."

If that woman were any colder, she could be an ice block. "I assure you, I'm not playing any game," Rachel answered smoothly. "I take everything I do quite seriously. And now, if you'll excuse me, Adam is waiting. We're going to discuss the budget."

After the meeting Rachel didn't see Adam all day. He'd briefly discussed the funds allotted for costumes, reminded her of the opening that night, then curtly dismissed her. He'd been so polite, so reserved, it was as if he'd forgotten all about last night. As if he'd forgotten how he'd ogled her legs yesterday at the rink.

As it turned out, Rachel didn't need to meet with Erika regarding the curriculum. Doreen had all the course outlines at her desk and was able to answer Rachel's questions. Rachel studied the outlines at her own desk backstage, making a conscious attempt to stay out of Erika's way. Except for lunch with Megan, it was a quiet day.

"Don't get used to it," Doreen said as Rachel was leaving. "Once classes start on Monday, you won't have time to breathe."

Back at the apartment, Rachel pulled out her mauve crepe suit from the closet. It was the dressiest outfit she had brought with her from Hartford. True, Erika had said the attire tonight was casual, but her definition of casual apparently differed from Rachel's. Today at work Erika had worn an expensive-looking rose silk dress.

Rachel had always liked the crepe suit. It hugged her in all the right places, sweeping low down the neckline. Not low enough to raise eyebrows, but low enough to get Erika's goat.

Her thoughts returned to the meeting in Adam's office. Fine, she thought. If he wanted to play it cool, it was perfectly all right with her—for now. Adam Wessler would come around...as soon as he saw how close she and Megan were becoming.

Be honest, she reprimanded herself. The neckline has nothing to do with Erika. Isn't it Adam's attention you're after? She dismissed the thought. All she wanted from him was friendship. It was part of the plan.

Really. Erika's scornful voice rose in her mind. Rachel dismissed that as well.

It was only after she slipped into the suit that she noticed the rip in the hemline. She groaned. She'd forgotten to pack her sewing kit. Handy with a needle and thread, she'd told Adam at the interview. What good was being handy if she didn't have the tools? She made a mental note to pick up a sewing kit at the fabric store in the morning. If she and Megan were going to work on Grace's costume, they'd need supplies.

In any case, there was no time for a fix-up job. She rummaged through the closet and finally decided on a chic black dress. No matter what Erika had said about the opening, there was no way Rachel intended to show up in normal working clothes, which for her meant a simple skirt and blouse. The black dress wasn't formal, but it was dressier than casual.

After searching for a place to park—she hadn't expected such a turnout for the opening—she finally found a spot at the side entrance where a large van had just pulled out. She looked up at the tower clock across the street. The search had cost her valuable minutes, but she still had twelve to spare. Running from the parking lot to the center, she remembered Erika's words. "The ceremony is at seven-thirty tomorrow evening. Please don't be late."

She ran through the open glass doors and once inside the reception area, stopped to catch her breath. "Rachel!" she heard Megan call. "Hurry, you're late!"

"What's the rush? The ceremony doesn't start until seven-thirty."

"Yes, but the reception started a half hour ago! You're missing the hors d'oeuvres. I came out here to look for you."

"A half hour ago! I thought—" Why was Megan so dressed up? And weren't those earrings a little too ornate? Down the long corridor several chattering women in full-length gowns were entering the conference room. "I can't go in there," Rachel whispered. "Look how I'm dressed. I didn't know it was a formal affair."

"But you have to! You're the new drama teacher! Dad even saved a place for you at our table. You should see it, there are flowers and even candles! You have to come!" Her face brightened. "I have an idea. Maybe there's a costume you can wear. Doreen and Erika go to the thrift shops all the time. Maybe they picked up something fancy. You know, in case we ever do a play about the *Titanic* or something like that."

I feel as if I'm on the *Titanic* right now, Rachel thought. And Erika is steering me straight for the iceberg. This wasn't just some casual get-together, and Rachel felt foolish. Foolish for not having inquired about tonight. Foolish for taking Erika at her word. "I don't think thrift shops sell formal wear," she said skeptically.

"They sell everything! Come on," Megan urged, taking Rachel's hand. "Let's give it a shot. You never know. You have a key to the dressing room, don't you?"

"Yes, but there's no time!"

"We still have—" she glanced at her watch "—ten whole minutes. Let's go!"

They raced down the hallway, hand in hand. A minute later Rachel found herself unlocking the door to the women's dressing room and, after that, the door to the walk-in closet at the back. "This is crazy," she said, ripping through old clothes. "These are rags! I'll never find anything here. And even if I did, what are the chances of it fitting?"

"Rachel, look!"

Hanging at the back of the closet was an exquisite emerald-green chiffon gown with long flowing sleeves and a sequined belt that tied on the side. Not only did it look expensive, it looked brand-new. Rachel pulled it off the hanger and looked for a label. There wasn't one. Could it be an original design? What was this marvelous creation doing here? And what on earth had it been doing in a thrift shop?

"It's gorgeous!" Megan gushed. "You'll look just like a princess!"

"It'll never fit. It looks too small."

"Try it on, please? You have to come to the reception. Please, Rachel? I'll wait outside in case my father comes looking for me. Ever since the burglaries started, he's been like a mother hen. He'll be worried if he doesn't find me."

Rachel looked at her daughter's eager face and sighed. She couldn't disappoint her.

Megan disappeared into the corridor. Rachel undressed and stepped into the gown. It was a little too tight across the bust, but other than that, it could have been made for her. Actually, she thought, pleased with the way it hugged her chest and hips, it wasn't too tight at all, if the desired effect was to get Erika's goat.

Or to get Adam to stand up and pay attention.

"Hurry, Rachel! Hurry!" came Megan's voice from the corridor. "Only four minutes left! Everyone's already inside!"

Rachel turned to look in the full-length mirror. The gown was lovely, even though it could have been a size larger. She looked down and realized, with relief, that she couldn't see her feet. Her black leather sling-backs might be fine for the dress she'd been wearing, but they'd never do for the showpiece she had on now.

She remembered her purse. That, too, was black leather. After removing her keys, she shoved the bag onto a shelf in the closet and locked the door.

One of bulbs over the mirror dimmed and began to make a buzzing noise. Startled, she looked up, then once again dropped her gaze on her reflection—and gasped. Glittering in the mirror, a heart-shaped pendant was suspended from a gold chain around her neck. Immediately her hand rose to her throat, but there was nothing there. Suddenly, with a pop, the overhead bulb died. She blinked, and the image in the mirror disappeared.

"Two minutes!" Megan called.

Get a hold of yourself, Rachel thought as she left the room. You're not seeing things, you're just nervous. What you saw was the flash from the bulb as it went out. She exhaled slowly to calm herself, but her hands were still trembling as she locked the door behind her.

"You look stunning!" Megan gushed. "You don't

look like a princess, you look like a queen! Except…''
She looked at Rachel thoughtfully. ''You need something around your neck. Why don't you wear my locket?
It has a picture of my mother in it, but nobody will see
it. I promised myself I'd never take it off, not even when
I sleep, not even when I take a bath, but this is an emergency. I'm sure my mother would understand.''

''No, don't take it off. A promise is a promise, even
if it's one you make to yourself.'' She paused. ''Maybe
this isn't such a good idea. This isn't my dress. Besides,
I have no place to put my keys.''

''It *is* your dress, Rachel. It was made for you. Give
me the keys. I'll hold them for you in my purse.''

Uncertain about the whole idea and still a little
shaken, Rachel followed Megan to the reception. The
divider between the two conference rooms had been
moved aside, and tables now filled the area. Megan took
Rachel's hand and led her to a table by the window.
''Sit here,'' she directed, ''between me and my father.''

At least a hundred people—all in formal attire—were
either seated at tables or standing in small groups, talking. Servers moved through the crowd with trays of hors
d'oeuvres. In the soft glow of candlelight, crystal and
silver gleamed from each table, arrangements of mixed
summer flowers adding to the elegant atmosphere.

Her stomach clenched. What if Erika recognized the
dress?

So what? What could the fashion-police officer do,
give her a ticket?

The look on Adam's face quickly dissolved her anxiety. ''Glad you could make it,'' he said, standing up,
his gaze lapping over her like a tongue. ''You look
lovely.''

Rachel couldn't remember the last time a man had

stood up when she'd entered the room. "Thank you. So do you. Handsome, I mean, not lovely." Darn. Why did he make her feel so flustered? It was as if she'd never seen a man in a tux before. He just happened to fill it out in ways she never thought possible.

"Ditto on the thank-you," he said.

Chivalrous almost to a fault, he pulled out her chair, and Rachel sat down. "It's wonderful in here," she said, trying to gather her composure. "When did all this take place?"

"The caterers arrived after work. It didn't take them long to—" His face went ashen.

"What is it?" she asked, alarmed. "You look as though you've seen a ghost."

"Where did you get that dress?"

She looked down at the green chiffon. "I, uh…"

"Don't be mad at her, Dad," Megan piped up from her chair. "It was my idea. I thought she'd look great in it, and she does, don't you think?"

"Come with me," he ordered, grabbing Rachel's arm. He practically hoisted her from her chair, and began pulling her from the table.

"Dad, what are you doing?" Megan cried out, a look of horror on her face.

When Rachel tried to break free of his hold, she was met with a look of contempt. "Let go of my arm," she hissed. "You're hurting me." When he wouldn't release her, she said, "People are looking."

There. That did it. Just as she'd thought, his public image took precedence over his anger. And just what was he so angry about? Maybe she shouldn't have taken the dress from wardrobe, but what was wrong with him, thinking he could manhandle her? She smoothed the dress and sat back down.

He continued to glare at her. "Do I have to drag you out of here or are you going to follow me quietly?"

Next to Megan, Erika was looking her way, a strange half curl twisting her mouth.

Had Erika set her up—twice? How could she have known that Rachel would take the gown? That woman is capable of anything, Rachel thought, returning a frozen smile.

Seething, Rachel rose from her chair and followed Adam into the corridor. "I'm sorry," she said, keeping her anger in check. "I'll change back into my own dress. I only did it because—" She stopped abruptly, knowing that Erika would only deny her part in the whole ordeal. Why would Adam take Rachel's word over that of his long-trusted friend?

"What in the world were you thinking?" he snarled. "Are you out of your mind? This dress belonged to my wife. Are you wearing her shoes, too?" He grabbed the fabric and lifted the gown to her knees.

"Stop that!" she protested, pulling the dress back down. "What in the world are *you* thinking? Are you out of *your* mind?"

"Let me tell you something, lady, I worshipped the ground she walked on, and no one, on this earth or anywhere else, can ever fill her shoes."

"Maybe I shouldn't have raided the costumes, but how dare you! And for your information, these are *my* shoes."

He stood back, momentarily rebuffed. "You think this gown is a costume? What, are you blind?"

"Adam."

He spun around. "Stay out of this, Doreen. This has nothing to do with you."

"It has everything to do with me. I recognized the

gown as soon as Rachel came into the room. This is all my fault. I'm the one who brought the dress to the center.''

"Would someone please tell me what's going on?" Rachel asked.

"Yes, tell us, Doreen," he said icily. "Tell us what's going on."

"I picked up the dress at the thrift shop on Birch Hill Road. I...I thought it would make a wonderful costume."

Adam's voice fell to a whisper. "This was the dress Cathy was going to wear for our anniversary. Our fifteenth wedding anniversary. She never got to wear it."

Doreen looked at him with sad eyes. "Adam, I'm so sorry. I didn't know—"

Adam cut her off with a fresh wave of anger. "I'm getting tired of your thoughtless interference, and I'm getting tired of these stupid mistakes. What's the matter with you? How could you have brought it here? How could you have been so insensitive?"

Doreen tried to speak, but a sob escaped instead. Her tears flowing freely, she backed away and ran off toward the theater.

"Talk about being insensitive," Rachel said hotly. "She told you she didn't know. This is just a misunderstanding. How could you have said those things?" She set off after Doreen, leaving Adam alone in the corridor.

Doreen was seated in the back row of the auditorium, crying softly. "He was caught by surprise," Rachel said, sitting down next to her. She placed a sympathetic hand on her arm. "He didn't mean what he said."

Doreen raised her head. "It's true. I'm an interfering old woman. It's just that his mother and I used to be

close, and he's always been like a son to me.'' She
dabbed at her wet cheeks. ''All I want to do is help, but
ever since Erika came into the picture, he's been pushing
me away. Oh, he still comes over with Megan and Evelyn for Sunday brunch. He does it for Megan, to give
her a sense of continuity. But soon all that will stop.
Erika knows I'm on to her, and she doesn't like me. I
can just imagine what she's been saying.''

''He's just upset. He never expected to see another
woman wearing his wife's clothes. He'll simmer down,
and once he realizes he overreacted, he'll apologize.''

''You don't understand,'' Doreen said through her
tears. ''Erika wants me out of the way. She wants *all* of
us out of the way. I've told Adam over and over what I
think of that gold-digging leech, but does he listen?
She's manipulative and scheming. Smart, too. Where
Adam is concerned, she knows exactly what buttons to
push. I'm terrified that one day she'll get her hands on
that pot of gold—and break Adam's heart in the process.''

Gold-digging leech? Pot of gold? How much could
the director of a community center possibly earn? Rachel
remembered Megan's comment, ''What's the use in having money if you don't spend it?'' Yesterday, in Adam's
car, Rachel hadn't given it a second thought.

''He's an attractive, single man,'' she said, trying to
make sense of what Doreen was saying. ''It stands to
reason that women will be clamoring at his door.''

''Clamoring? Erika is a one-woman attack force!
Mark my words, she won't quit her post until she's married him and gone through every red cent.''

Rachel was baffled. She'd been to Adam's house. Although tastefully decorated, it wasn't anything someone
might find showcased in *Homes and Gardens.* And what

about his car? Yet Doreen and Megan spoke about him as if he had money to burn.

Doreen must have read the confusion on Rachel's face. "Adam is a modest man," she explained. "Even though he inherited a tidy nest egg from his father, he doesn't like to put on airs. But the nest egg isn't what has Erika drooling. Everyone knows that Adam stands to inherit the bulk of his father's estate, and let me tell you, it makes that nest egg look like lunch money."

Evidently the private investigator had not done all his homework. He might have a penchant for words, Rachel thought, but if he'd spent more time investigating the essentials than he'd spent digging up tidbits like Adam's favorite flavor of soda, she wouldn't be sitting with her mouth hanging open as she listened to what Doreen was saying.

And Adam's inheritance *was* an essential piece of information. It was a relief to know that, financially, Megan would be taken care of. As for Erika, Rachel now knew just what kind of adversary she was dealing with.

"Erika is waiting for Adam's mother to die," she said, shuddering.

Doreen snorted. "No, I think Erika's getting a little tired of the waiting game. I told you, she's smart. She knows that the money will be his once he exercises his power of attorney. She's urging Adam to have Evelyn committed."

Rachel stayed silent, mulling over Doreen's words. What good was all that money to Erika if she and Adam were just friends? Adam had made it clear to Rachel that he wasn't interested in marrying again. The man had too many responsibilities. But what if these responsibilities were to conveniently disappear? "Erika wants to send

Megan away, as well, to a school in New York," Rachel said, the pieces of the puzzle coming together.

"You've got that right. Erika wants his money, not his daughter. That poor child. Why can't Adam see what's going on? Sometimes I could just throttle him."

"I still don't understand how the dress wound up in a thrift shop. Erika couldn't have planned this whole mess, but why do I get the feeling that she was involved?"

Doreen let out a sigh. "A few days ago Erika and I were at the house, and she started in on him again. She told him it was time to get rid of Cathy's personal belongings, and this time he didn't argue. He asked her to come by the next day when he'd be out of the house. It would have caused him too much pain to be there."

"And she took the clothes to the thrift shop."

"I remember Adam explicitly telling her to donate them to charity, but Erika is Erika, and even though the thrift shops don't pay well, a buck is a buck. She thinks she's so savvy, but it's obvious she had no idea what that dress was worth."

"And never having seen it before, you picked it up."

"There you have it," Doreen said, rising. She smoothed her hair with her fingers. "I suppose we ought to join the reception."

Rachel took her arm as they headed back to the conference area. "You go on in," she said, giving her a reassuring hug. "I'm going to change and then head home."

"For what it's worth," Doreen said, "I think you look splendid."

Adam was standing in the doorway. "I agree," he said.

* * *

He'd felt lower than a snail. He knew there was no way anyone could have known about the dress, but he'd been unable to keep his emotions in check. It was as if, for one brief moment, Cathy had come back to him, and when he'd realized she hadn't, he'd allowed his disappointment to rise to a scalding anger. Anger at himself for his flight of fancy. Anger at Cathy for dying.

He'd apologized over and over to Doreen and Rachel. What else could a man do after behaving in such a way? "Don't go," he'd said to Rachel. And she hadn't.

After the conference area had been cleared for dancing, he asked Erika to take Mark and Sylvia Porter, the couple who had donated a substantial sum to the center, on a tour of the grounds. She left the room—reluctantly, he noted with puzzlement—and with Rachel at his side, he set out to mingle with the guests.

He had to admit, Rachel was a vision in the dress. From their admiring stares he knew that everyone in the room seemed to think so, too.

He asked her to dance. She smells like roses, he thought, as they moved across the makeshift dance floor. He lowered his hands around her tiny waist and could have sworn he felt her tremble. When he dipped her, she laughed nervously, the sound reminding him of little jingling bells.

Why was she so nervous? Wasn't this what she wanted? All evening she'd been doing that thing women did whenever they were interested, tossing her hair off her shoulders as though she didn't have a care in the world.

He found it enchanting, and as much as he tried to deny it, she was getting under his skin. It was probably the champagne, he figured, as the three-piece band slowed down the music. It always affected him this way. He hadn't had champagne since—

He pulled away.

"What's the matter?" she asked, looking up at him with questioning eyes. Large emerald eyes that matched the shade of the gown. "Don't you like the music?"

The lump in his throat was the size of a golf ball. The last time he had tasted champagne was the night before his fifteenth anniversary. The night before the accident. Megan was at a sleepover at a friend's house, and he and Cathy had decided to start the celebration early, at home, just the two of them.

"Let's get some air," he said gruffly. He took Rachel's arm and led her through the crowd.

They made their way into the corridor, toward the stairwell. "Where are we going?" she asked, hesitancy in her voice. He didn't answer. On the second floor he opened the two glass doors that led outside to the balcony.

A spray of light invited them to step forward. Overhead a blanket of stars like thousands of diamonds glittered in the night sky.

"It's breathtaking out here," she said, leaning against the railing.

In the moonlight he could see the curves of her body beneath the gown. He turned his eyes away and gazed up at the sky. "This place isn't open to the public yet. Sometimes I come here to escape."

"Memories?"

"Ah, hell, you must think I'm a real wimp. Here I am, alone with a beautiful woman, both of us gazing at the sky, and I'm taking a walk down memory lane."

"You miss your wife," she said simply.

"We used to look at the stars for hours. Sometimes

we didn't even speak.'' He felt the pain sear through him. ''I'm sorry, Rachel. I don't want to bore you with this. I'll take you back downstairs.''

''You're not boring me,'' she whispered.

He lowered his gaze and met her stare, the look in her eyes melting away the last of his defenses. Seeing her in that dress had opened up floodgates, and he couldn't hold back the grief. ''After the accident,'' he said in a thick voice, ''I was a madman. I'd get up in the morning and ask myself why I even bothered. I'd either bury myself in work or in a bottle of scotch. I knew I was trying to bury myself along with her, but I forced myself to get my act together. I had Megan to think of. And then my father died, and I had to take care of my mother, too. I was so busy I didn't even notice the days passing. I didn't even notice that Cathy was fading until one day, when I was going through our old high school annual, I tried to picture her face, and I couldn't...I...'' He swallowed hard. ''Details I once knew by heart were no longer there. Her hazel eyes were speckled with gold, but I couldn't picture them in my mind. She's fading, and I can't do anything about it.''

''It's hard to let go,'' she said. ''I know.''

She caressed the side of his face and something in him snapped. ''God help me,'' he whispered, ''I wasn't thinking about her when you first came into the room, and I wasn't thinking about her when we started to dance.'' Before he could stop himself, he pulled her to him with a violence that took him by surprise, and crashed his mouth down on hers. Her lips were moist and warm, awakening something in him he'd thought was gone forever. When she tried to break free of his hold, her resistance only added to his fire.

He released his lips to seek the creamy flesh of her

neck. "Cathy," he murmured, taking in the sweet perfume of her hair. "Cathy."

He froze, the sound of his own voice sobering him. She backed away and stared at him wordlessly.

"Go ahead," he said, grimacing. "Tell me I'm a jerk."

"Okay, you're a jerk."

"Why don't you slap me or something? I deserve it."

"It's okay," she said in a shaky voice. "I understand."

But it wasn't okay. Even though he'd stupidly called her by his late wife's name, it wasn't Cathy he'd been thinking of. It wasn't Cathy he'd wanted to devour with his lips.

"Rachel…" he began, then stopped. What could he say that would explain what had happened—what he was feeling—when he himself didn't know?

His cell phone buzzed and he took it out of his pocket. Saved by the bell, he thought absurdly. Just what was it he needed saving from?

He stepped away from the railing to take the call. A few moments later he returned to her side. "That was Paula. It seems there's been another crisis. It's nothing major, but I'm going home. My mother's having another one of her spells."

"What can I do to help?"

Rachel looked so earnest, he had to resist the urge to take her in his arms again. "You can give me a lift," he answered. "Ethel's back in the shop. Erika drove me over here, but I need her to stay until the reception is over. She can drive Megan home later."

That was a crock and he knew it. The important segment of the opening was over and any number of people could take him home.

"I'd be happy to drive you," she said. "I have to get my keys from Megan. My bag's in the dressing room. What about the gown? Do I have time to change?"

He managed a small smile. "Keep the gown. You wear it well."

Chapter Five

"Why didn't you want Megan to come back with us?" Rachel asked as she pulled out of the parking lot.

"Something's happened to Cinnamon. We might have to take her to the vet, and I don't want Megan worrying."

Rachel glanced at him in the passenger seat. "I thought the crisis had something to do with your mother."

"Rachel, please keep your eyes on the road."

She tightened her grip on the steering wheel and stared out the windshield. He hadn't replied to her remark. It was obvious that he had retreated into his shell. Hard to believe that just minutes ago he had practically ravished her on the balcony. Adam Wessler was an emotional yo-yo.

When she'd entered the conference area, his pleasure had been undeniable. When he'd realized that the dress she was wearing had belonged to Cathy, he'd been en-raged. Then, just like that, he'd turned into a sex fiend. And what about this morning at the meeting in his office? Why had he been so distant? She was getting tired of his hot-and-cold moods.

She had no intention of keeping the dress. She would take it to one of the local charities. This was what he'd originally wanted. *I should have changed out of it before we left,* she thought as she turned onto Birch Hill Road. It was too small, and she felt constricted.

She wriggled uncomfortably in the driver's seat. The material across her chest pulled so tight, she was sure it would burst wide open, giving Adam an eyeful. As she braked for a red light, her hem caught under her shoe, and she skidded to a stop.

"Rachel, be careful!" Adam commanded. "I'd like to get home alive."

Was he thinking of the accident that had taken Cathy's life? Of course he was. He'd been thinking about Cathy all evening. Spurred on by the dress, he'd been deluded by fantasy, his desire sparked by his late wife's memory.

True, Rachel had felt sorry for him, but she had to admit, she had also seen his reaction as an opportunity. There was no way she'd allow the kiss to lead anywhere, but wouldn't he regard her compassion as a positive quality? Wouldn't it work right into her plan to imbed herself in his life, thereby ensuring a place for herself in Megan's?

But something had happened, something she hadn't figured on. When his eyes had burned a path right through to her soul, she'd liked it. She'd liked the way he'd encircled her waist, the way he'd crushed her against him and kissed her.

So why had she tried to pull away?

She knew the answer. Romance was only an illusion, a temporary distraction that would only complicate her plan. In any case, the last thing she wanted—the last thing any woman wanted—was to be a replacement for someone's wife.

Really, she thought, hearing Erika's voice in her head. *I don't know what kind of game you think you're playing.*

She pulled into his driveway, catching a glimpse of his profile. He looked so forlorn, so worried, she wanted to reach out and touch him. Stop right there, she told herself. That's how it had started, out on the balcony when she'd caressed the side of his face.

No, it had started at the rink, she realized. She'd always had a soft spot for a man who needed healing. A man in need. Tonight on the balcony, Adam had made his need quite obvious, but that was one particular need she had no intention of fulfilling.

She turned off the ignition. In a flash he was out of the car, coming around to her door. Always the gentleman, she thought, even in a crisis. He unlocked the front door to the house and stepped aside, allowing her to enter before him.

"Adam!" his mother called out. "Will you please tell this woman that I'm perfectly capable of doing the laundry?"

Evelyn was sitting on the couch, sipping water through a straw. Last night she'd worn a terry cloth bathrobe, but tonight all she had on was a long cotton nightgown. Loosely draped over her body, it accentuated her delicate frame. Her thin arms and legs jutted out from beneath, and Rachel was shocked by her frailty.

"I'm so sorry you had to leave the gala," Paula said, looking up. She was seated next to Evelyn, holding the glass close to the other woman's lips. ''Evelyn's still a little shaky, but she's calmed down. It's Cinny I'm worried about. She won't even let me near her.''

Curled up in the wing chair next to the couch, Cinnamon was whimpering. Adam approached her and petted her behind her ears. ''Poor little Cinny. Have you had a fright?'' He looked over at Paula. ''She's seems okay. Try petting her now.''

''Here, give me the glass,'' Rachel said as Paula rose from the couch. ''I'll take over.'' She sat down next to Evelyn, and with a tremulous hand Evelyn maneuvered the straw back into her mouth, her fingers as thin as matchsticks.

Paula cautiously approached the wing chair. ''There's a good puppy,'' she said, stroking the spaniel gently. ''Feeling better now?''

''Hello?'' Evelyn said between sips of water. ''Am I invisible?''

Adam chuckled. ''Now, Mom,'' he said warmly, ''don't get in a tizzy.'' He bent low and gave her a quick peck on her cheek.

Just like that, she was mollified, her eyes glowing with affection. Rachel was impressed by how quickly Adam could turn his mother's mood around—although she suspected that Evelyn's complacency wouldn't last.

Evelyn took the glass from Rachel, and with a slow, deliberate movement placed it on the coffee table. ''There, now,'' she said with pride. ''You see? I'm not an invalid.''

Adam smiled at her with tenderness, then turned his attention back to Paula. ''What happened?''

''Like I told you on the phone, Cinnamon took a spin in the dryer.'' Paula's hand flew to her mouth. ''I'm so sorry, Adam, I didn't mean to sound flippant.''

"My God!" Rachel cried. "Did you say the dryer?"

"She couldn't have been in there for more than a second or two," Paula said. "And the towels must have prevented her from getting banged around."

"How did she get in there?" Rachel asked, perplexed.

"After I saw Evelyn off to bed, I decided to take a bath. I thought Evelyn was asleep. If I'd thought she was awake, I never would have left her alone. I never would have…" Paula's voice trailed off, guilt etched across her lined face.

"You can't be expected to watch her every minute," Adam said. "Don't blame yourself. I'm just grateful you got to Cinny in time."

"I heard a noise from the laundry room and I went downstairs to investigate," Paula continued. "And there was Evelyn, turning on the dryer." She smiled sadly at Rachel. "Sometimes she does things backward. Apparently, she decided to dry the laundry before washing it."

"Don't talk about me as if I'm not here," Evelyn snapped.

"Come along, Evelyn," Paula said, taking her arm. "Adam is home now. I'll help you back to your room."

"Stay away from me!" Evelyn pulled away from Paula and grabbed Adam's sleeve. "I know what's she's been up to! She's been trying to kill me—she's been poisoning my tea! You have to fire her!" Her voice lowered. "I'll let you in on a little secret. I'm smarter than she is. When she's not looking, I pour it all down the toilet."

"Now, Evelyn," Paula said, "you know you don't drink tea. You told me you don't like it. Let me help you back upstairs."

"Of course I don't drink tea! Why would I drink

something that's been poisoned? Stay away from me! I want Beth to take me upstairs.''

"This is Rachel,'' Adam said patiently. "Don't you remember? She was here last night.''

"It's okay, Adam,'' Rachel said, her heart thumping. There it was again. *Beth.* Her mother's name. "I'll go with her.''

"No, I'll take her,'' Adam said. "Come on, Mom. You're upset. Come upstairs and I'll tell you all about tonight. Remember the opening I told you about? Everyone asked about you, and I told them how you helped get Megan ready. Everyone loved the earrings.''

Evelyn turned to Rachel. "Adam's father gave me those earrings on my birthday,'' she said with sudden clarity. "Aren't they beautiful?'' Her eyes suddenly filled with tears. "He's been gone for over a year now. It's been hard on Adam, having to take care of me. I know I'm a burden, but he never complains. Take care of him, Rachel. He's a good man.''

Then, as suddenly as it had appeared, the lucidity in her tone vanished. "Is that a new dress, dear? Maybe I can let it out—you've put on a little weight. I'm glad. You were always too thin. Good night, Cathy.''

Adam's wife must have been as thin as a pencil, Rachel thought. I'm only a size six. Once again she was struck by Evelyn's frailty, which was even more apparent when Adam took her arm to help her up from the couch. "Good night, Evelyn,'' she said with forced cheer, and watched as they disappeared up the stairs.

Paula motioned for Rachel to follow her into the kitchen. "Would you like some coffee? Or maybe some tea?'' she added mischievously.

"Just water, thank you.'' Rachel hesitated before

speaking again. "Paula, how long has Adam's mother been like this?"

Paula took a pitcher from the refrigerator and poured them each a glass of water. "It started about four years ago. She'd forget where she parked the car, where she put the keys, things like that. Things, Lord knows, I'm guilty of myself. But a year ago, when Adam's father died, Evelyn started going downhill fast. Adam insisted she move in with him, and that's when he hired me. But now…"

"What is it?" Rachel asked, reading the concern in the older woman's eyes. "She's not sick, is she?"

"Sick? Oh, you mean outside of the Alzheimer's. No, thank heavens. But she's deteriorating rapidly, and she occasionally has seizures. She had the first one two months ago when she fell and fractured her wrist. Megan was reading in her room and I was preparing dinner when we heard a crash. We found Evelyn on the floor, shaking with convulsions."

"My God," Rachel said. "That poor woman. And Megan must have been traumatized."

Paula frowned. "I'm afraid Adam has some serious decisions to make. I was a registered nurse before I retired, but Evelyn's condition is growing beyond my expertise. I take care of the house, but that's not why he hired me. He hired me to take care of his mother."

"You certainly have your work cut out for you," Rachel said sympathetically.

"Adam helps out a lot. Evelyn was right when she said that he's a good man. And Megan's a real sweetheart. She's very devoted to her grandmother. She helps out, too."

"What about Erika?"

Paula let out a scornful laugh. "Erika Johnson? I don't

think so. Sure, she comes over, makes a big pretense about helping, but all she really does is upset Evelyn. Oh, I know Evelyn talks as though she hates me, too, but it's just an act. For the most part, we get along fine. I knew her before this all started. In the old days, before the Alzheimer's.''

''You were friends?'' Rachel asked, suddenly alarmed. Had Paula known Rachel's mother, too?

''Acquaintances. Like Adam's father, my husband was a lawyer. He had a small practice, nothing like Frank Wessler's, but we attended the same social functions. Fundraisers, that sort of thing.''

A loud yelp came from the living room, and Paula and Rachel ran out of the kitchen. On the couch, Cinnamon was wriggling pathetically. Rachel looked at Paula helplessly. ''What's the matter with her? What's happening?''

''My God, she's having a seizure!''

''What can we do?'' Rachel implored, her hysteria rising. As she spoke, the convulsions ceased.

''It's over,'' Paula said, relief in her voice. ''After Evelyn has a seizure, she's tired, but she's all right. Nevertheless I think Cinny should be checked out. I used to be a nurse, not a veterinarian.'' Gingerly she picked up the dog and handed her to Rachel. ''There's a twenty-four-hour clinic in Danbury. Here, take her to the car, and I'll get Adam.''

Rachel carried Cinnamon to her car and placed her on the passenger seat. The spaniel lifted her head and looked up with large, trusting eyes. ''Adam is coming,'' Rachel said, stroking her silky ears. Cinnamon perked up as if she understood.

A moment later Adam was sitting next to Rachel, Cinnamon on his lap. ''I need directions,'' Rachel said, looking at him expectantly. He rattled them off, then began cooing to the dog as if she were a baby.

In spite of her concern, Rachel felt reassured. Cinnamon would be all right as long as Adam was with her. He had a way about him. Soothing. Calming.

Just who was the healer? Rachel wondered. She or Adam?

Rachel Hartwell had to be the most perplexing woman he'd ever met. On the drive to the clinic she'd chatted on about the joys of Middlewood and how glad she was to be a part of the community, but whenever he'd questioned her about her life, she'd tensed up tighter than a cat in a yard full of dogs.

And she was wily, he thought as he sat next to her in the waiting room. Somehow she'd managed to turn the conversation around to his own life. She'd asked him what it was like growing up in Middlewood, about his family, his upbringing, and before he knew it, he'd started spilling his guts. Again.

Not once did she bring up what had happened on the balcony. Why wasn't she angry? Didn't women like to rehash these things ad nauseam? If he had addressed Erika by his wife's name, she would have given him a tongue-lashing—and they were just friends.

Friends. The way he and Rachel were friends. Or were they? All evening she'd been coming on to him, doing that hair thing, smiling up at him as if he were the only man in the room, but when he'd kissed her, she'd tried to pull away.

Fine. Just friends they would remain. An unsettling thought occurred to him. When exactly had he and this stranger become friends? He must have been asleep at the time.

Something else gnawed at his insides, something that had nagged at him ever since he'd picked up her résumé. Why would anyone leave a secure, cushy job in a private school to work for less pay in a small town?

True, like Rachel, he had left a secure position to work here, but it had been a step up, not down. Not that he needed the money. His father had left him and his mother a tidy sum. Adam frowned, remembering when he'd told his father he didn't want to go to law school and become a partner in the firm. When Adam had told him he intended to be a teacher, his father had been less than pleased.

As much as he hated to admit it, Adam knew that his father had been right. Not about the value of teaching — Adam admired, even envied, those who were capable— but about making the wrong career choice. Over the years he had come to realize that his talent lay in organization, his heart in the arts. He became active in the community, coordinating all the town's festivities, and his efforts hadn't gone unnoticed. When the town council approached him with this job, he'd grabbed it, knowing that being the community center's director would allow him the creative outlet he longed for.

As for Rachel, it didn't make sense. What could working at the center give her that she didn't already have? She'd come up with a number of reasons, but he suspected that all of them had been fabricated solely for his benefit.

"Mr. Wessler?" A woman in a white smock smiled at him from behind a counter. "We're ready for Cinnamon."

After a thorough examination, Dr. Warner pulled off her plastic gloves with a snap and said, "She seems fine. Without doing extensive testing, we can't be sure what triggered the seizure, or if in fact it was a seizure. I'm hoping that it was just an isolated event caused by the trauma.''

"What if it's not isolated?" Adam asked.

"We can't administer treatment unless she has more episodes. Generally speaking, treatment is only necessary for animals having one or more a month. Take her home, Mr. Wessler, and keep a close watch on her. Try to keep her quiet. If she has another seizure, remain calm. Loud or sudden noises might make it worse.''

Adam scooped up Cinnamon. "Thank you, Doctor. Let's hope we won't have to make a return visit."

"Should we tell Megan?" Rachel asked on the drive back to the house.

"That poor kid's been through so much already, I hate to worry her. But I suppose I'll have to say something. She'll need to be on the lookout for any abnormal behavior. And I'll have to watch Megan. I don't know how this will affect her.''

"You always speak about her as if she's disturbed. What's going on, Adam?"

Cinnamon wiggled in his lap. As though wanting to answer Rachel's question, she lifted her head and barked. "Shh, girl," Adam soothed. "The doctor said you have to stay quiet." Cinnamon looked up at him inquiringly, then settled down on his lap.

Adam sighed. "Until two months ago, even though Megan had been aware of Evelyn's condition, she'd always acted as though it didn't bother her. They used to play together as if they were both kids. It was really sweet, seeing them together like that. Then everything changed. My mother had her first seizure, and the possibility that Megan might lose her grandmother became a frightening reality.''

Rachel pulled into the driveway. "There's more, isn't there?' she said, turning off the ignition.

He made no move to leave the car. "Oh, there's more, all right. When I arrived home, the ambulance was already there. Later that night, after I got back from the hospital, I went upstairs to check on Megan, but her bed was empty. I was frantic. I was about to call the police, when she came in through her bedroom window. I drilled her about her whereabouts, but she wouldn't talk, and the next morning I learned there'd been another robbery." He remembered what Dr. Warner had said about Cinny and added, "Megan's sneaking out wasn't an isolated event. I'm almost positive it's still going on. But that's not what's scaring me to death. What about the burglaries? She promised she had nothing to do with them, but what if she's lying?"

"That's crazy! Megan is not a thief. Look, I'm not excusing her for sneaking out, but I can understand. This is her way of lashing out. First she loses her mother, then she comes face-to-face with the possibility of losing her grandmother."

"You sound as if you're speaking from experience."

"I was close to my grandmother."

There it was again, that tight-lipped expression. He waited for her to continue, and when she didn't, he said, "Rachel, talk to me. I thought we were becoming friends. Friends talk to each other."

"What do you mean? We talk."

"You know exactly what I mean. All evening you've been turning the conversation away from yourself."

She shrugged. "I already told you, my mother and I moved around a lot. When we weren't moving, my mother was away on tour. My grandmother came and took care of me."

"No father?"

When she didn't answer, he leaned against the car door, studying her guarded face in the glow from the street lamp. He didn't want to seem as though he was prying, but dammit, he was curious.

Prying. Now that was funny, not that he was laughing. She'd had no trouble prying *him* open. He couldn't believe the things he'd talked about on the drive to the vet. For example, his relationship with his father. Frank Wessler had been a good friend to his peers, a model citizen in the community, but to his family he'd been exacting and rigid. Lavish with money yet miserly with affection, he'd ruled the family with an iron hand. He'd never assaulted Adam or his mother, but growing up, Adam had felt his father's coldness as acutely as if he'd been slapped.

Adam hadn't thought about this in years, let alone talked about it. What was it about Rachel that sent his mouth into overdrive?

"Come in for a while," he said, ignoring the voice in his head. The voice that warned him to stay clear of this mysterious woman from Hartford. "Megan should be home by now. I know she'll want to see you."

In spite of his reservations, there was something about the new drama teacher that intrigued him. Something mysterious yet oddly familiar.

"You should have let me come with you."

Scowling, her hands on her hips, Megan stood in the entranceway to the living room. Rachel was reminded of the first time she'd laid eyes on her. It seemed like eons ago, when in fact it had happened only yesterday.

"We've already been over this, Megan," Adam said patiently. "I didn't want to worry you."

"I'm not a baby," she retorted. "You don't have to protect me. Did *she* talk you out of my coming along?"

Rachel felt as though a rock had been lodged in her chest. Megan spoke as if she resented her. Apparently, she'd abandoned her matchmaking scheme. What had caused the sudden turn-around?

"Erika said that Cinny might be dying! Can you imagine how I felt? You said that Grandma was having another one of her spells, but that it wasn't serious. How could you lie to me? And how could you take Cinny to the vet without me?" She cast a hostile glare at Rachel. "It was probably *your* idea. Don't think I don't know what's going on! You don't give a hoot about Cinny. You just used her to get close to my father. I know what you're after. And why are you still wearing my mother's dress? You're too fat for it, anyway! Dad, make her give it back!"

"That's enough, Megan. I think an apology is in order."

"I won't apologize! Why should I? She's the one who should apologize."

"You're right, sweetheart," Rachel said. "Cinny is your dog, and you should have come with us. I'm sorry, Megan. We were wrong."

Megan wasn't appeased. "No, I'm the one who was wrong," she spat. "Wrong about you. And don't call me sweetheart." She spun around and ran upstairs.

"Let me go to her, Adam," Rachel said, noting Adam's frustration. "Maybe I can get to the bottom of what's bothering her."

He nodded slowly. "All right, go. But troubled or not, it's no excuse for the way she's acting. Sometimes that girl drives me crazy."

The door to Megan's room was open, and tentatively

Rachel entered. Megan was sprawled on her bed, flipping through a magazine. "What do you want?" she asked without looking up. "I take that back. I know what you want."

"I want us to be friends," Rachel said quietly.

"Yeah, right. Friends." Megan leafed through a few more pages before speaking again. "These magazines are so stupid. How to lose ten pounds in a week. How to dress up your wardrobe without spending a dime. How to get a man to pay more attention. Do you believe this garbage?" She looked up at Rachel. "You must have the same magazines as I do."

"Actually, I do," she said, ignoring Megan's innuendoes. "And you're right. They're stupid."

"Yeah? So why do you buy them?"

"They're a diversion, an escape from the real world. But you can't believe everything you read."

"You can't believe everything people tell you, either," Megan said testily.

She means me, Rachel thought. Had Erika said something negative to Megan? "Did anyone say anything to make you angry? I thought we were getting along so well, but now you're acting as if I'm your enemy."

Megan sat up and put down the magazine. "That's another thing. Why were we getting along at all? You act as if I'm somebody important. Somebody special. But you don't even know me!"

Rachel sat down on the edge of the bed, wishing fervently that she could tell her daughter the truth. But it was too soon. Adam would send her away. But maybe she could tell Megan part of what was in her heart. "I feel as if I've always known you. Maybe it's because I always wanted a daughter, and I always imagined she'd be just like you."

"And why is that?" Megan asked suspiciously. "Wait, don't tell me. It must be because I'm such a joy to have around. Ask my father. He'll tell you. He'll tell you about how he thinks I run around with gangs and criminals, breaking into people's houses."

"Do you?"

"What do you think?"

"I think no."

"Yeah, well, at least *someone* believes me." Megan hugged her knees to her chest, all traces of her anger gone. "Can I ask you something?"

Rachel leaned over and smoothed back Megan's hair. "Anything."

"You said you always wanted a daughter. What would you name her?"

Rachel hesitated. "Katie."

"Really? When I was a little girl, I had a doll named Katie. She was my very favorite doll in the whole world! You know what I think? I think we must have been soul sisters in another lifetime. Do you believe in all that? I do. I believe there's a string that connects people's hearts, a long silver thread that connects people from one lifetime to the next."

"I believe that love lives on forever," Rachel answered, blinking back a sudden threat of tears.

Can you feel it? she'd whispered to her unborn child, resting her hands on the curve of her belly. *Can you feel it flowing down my arms, through my fingers, from my heart all the way to yours?*

"Forever," Megan repeated as though the word held magic. "No one really dies, do they? I mean, not in our hearts. That's what Dad always says." She paused. "I'm a real brat, aren't I? I'm sorry I said those mean things to you. And I don't think you're fat. We're still going to work on my costume tomorrow, aren't we?''

"You bet we are. Why don't I swing by tomorrow around noon? If your father says it's okay, I'll take you out for lunch.''

"Cool! Rachel?''

"What is it, sweetheart?''

"It's true. You can't believe everything people tell you. Some people, anyway.''

"I don't know how you do it,'' Adam said. "You must have a magic touch.''

Rachel picked up her purse from the coffee table. "I told Megan I'd come by around noon tomorrow. I'd like to take her to lunch before we start on her costume. Is that all right?''

"That's fine. I appreciate all the time you're spending with her.'' His eyes flashed with sudden curiosity. "Can I ask you something?''

She smiled. He sounded just like Megan. "What is it, Adam?''

"How is it you never married? I would think someone would have snatched you up a long time ago. And you get along so well with kids. Don't you want a family of your own?''

What was the harm in telling him about her marriage? A lot of people were divorced. There was no way he could connect her situation to her past. "I *was* married, briefly.''

"What happened? Ah, there I go again, prying. I'm sorry. Sorry for being nosy and sorry about your marriage.''

"Don't be, on both counts. As for my marriage, sometimes things just don't work out. It wasn't anyone's fault.'' But there had been more to it than that. She'd been unable to return the love her husband had offered, and she hadn't stopped him from leaving.

"But you kept your married name."

Her mouth flew open. "How…how did you know that?"

"I didn't. I guessed. And now you've confirmed my suspicion."

"Of all the low-down, dirty tricks! Why didn't you just ask me?"

"Would you have answered? Who are you, Rachel? What are you running from?"

"What is this? An inquisition?" She turned around and headed for the door. With just one long stride, he was behind her, spinning her around by her arm.

"Still running, Rachel? What are you afraid of? It can't be me. Do I look like an ax murderer?"

"Don't be ridiculous. And don't interrogate me. This isn't your business, Adam."

"It *is* my business," he said, his head so close to hers, she could feel his breath on her neck. "Somehow you've managed to put my daughter under your spell, and if I had any sense at all, I'd tell you to pack your bags and leave."

"Why don't you? If you're so convinced I'm some kind of criminal, why don't you fire me?" Shut up, Rachel. Shut up! What if he did just that? What if he fired her? Ordered her to pack up and leave, as he'd said. Ordered her out of Megan's life forever.

"You're no criminal, but you're hiding something, and trust me, sooner or later I'll find out what it is. So you might as well own up now."

She choked back her anger, forcing herself to calm

down. "Please, Adam, let it go. I'm not ready. I'm not—"

"Not ready for what? Not ready to let me in on your little secret?" His voice softened. "Not ready to let someone into your life?"

She stood there, paralyzed. He was going to kiss her again, and she knew she wouldn't resist. "Don't," she said weakly, her arms hanging helplessly at her side. God help her, she wanted him. Against all reasoning, she wanted him.

This time he eased her into the circle of his arms instead of pulling her roughly. This time his kiss was slow and drugging, and she didn't try to break away.

"This isn't happening," she murmured. "It can't be real."

"This isn't real?" He moved his lips down her neck, tracing an erotic path. "What about this?" he breathed into her hair. His fingers traveled a slow trail to the small of her back, sending little shivers down her spine. "Is this an illusion, too? Tonight, when I first saw you," he whispered, "I thought *you* weren't real. I thought I was dreaming. But you're not an illusion. You're as real and soft as the fabric of your dress."

Her dress or Cathy's? she wondered.

This time she was the one who froze.

The chill she felt was real, all right, and it had come over her in the nick of time. "I'm not her," she said angrily, pulling away.

He smiled at her crookedly. "I knew we'd get around to that. The famous balcony scene. Look, it was just a dumb mistake. I called you Cathy out of habit. It doesn't mean anything. You're the first woman—"

"Stop right there, Adam. I'm not interested in your

explanation. The next time you have a delusion, I suggest you call a therapist. I'm not Cathy.''

He stared at her blankly, then drew back. ''I know who you *aren't,* Rachel. What I don't know is who you *are.*''

Chapter Six

"How about lunch at the Café St. Gabriel?"

Adam turned to stare at Erika. "Excuse me?"

"Adam! You haven't been listening to a word I've been saying. You've been preoccupied since you got into the car."

"Sorry. Sure, we can have lunch, if you want."

"Try not to look so excited."

Adam grinned apologetically. "Sorry," he repeated. "You know I always have a good time with you. Thanks for the lift, by the way. Look, why don't we have brunch instead? It's only eleven-thirty, but I'm hungry now. I didn't have breakfast. We'll eat before we pick up Ethel. That way we only have to take one car."

Adam knew that on Saturdays the Café St. Gabriel in Ridgefield didn't open until one. The truth was, he didn't want to go there. He pictured the decor of the fashionable French restaurant—the floor-to-ceiling fieldstone fireplace, the heavy oak beams that lined the ceiling, the secluded outdoor courtyard where a violinist provided a backdrop of light classical music—and felt a pang. As if it were yesterday, he recalled the first time he had gone there with Cathy, the New Year's Eve before their wedding. They'd snuggled inside on the plush velvet love seat by the fire, talking about their future—the kind of house they wanted, the lifestyle they'd follow, the children they'd have. "A boy for you," she'd said, "and a girl for me." He smiled inwardly, remembering her cheerfulness. It was a cheerfulness that had endured throughout her life. Even when they'd found out that she couldn't conceive, she'd remained undaunted, suggesting adoption.

Erika's voice, heavy with disappointment, broke through his reverie. "The café doesn't open until later. I was looking forward to a quiet meal out in the courtyard. Something intimate…romantic…"

Adam opened his mouth to speak, then closed it. Intimate? Romantic? Where had that come from? After all this time, Erika was talking romance? Women. No matter how long he lived, he would never figure them out. Not once had Erika even hinted that they take their relationship to the next level.

Or had she? He had to admit, he was no expert in this area, having been out of the dating scene for so long. In truth, he'd never really been part of it. According to today's standards he'd be considered a dinosaur. How many men had been with only one woman? How many men would admit it?

He glanced over at Erika, and for the first time that day—maybe the first time ever—noticed what she was wearing. The backless red halter top didn't leave much to the imagination. Wasn't she cold? It had rained again earlier this morning, and unlike last night, the downfall had left a chill in the air. He'd noticed a jacket lying on the back seat, but something warned him against suggesting that she put it on. Instinctively he knew she would be offended.

Maybe he was more in tune with the way women thought than he believed.

Or maybe not. His thoughts drifted to Rachel. Okay, maybe he was more than a little out of tune; maybe he wasn't even in the orchestra. At his house, Rachel had made it clear that she had no intention of going where he'd been headed, but had he listened? Sure, she'd rebuffed him, but she'd been interested, all right. There were signals a woman put out whether she realized it or not. It had taken him a while to get it through his skull that, interested or not, when she said *don't,* she meant it. Well, if that was how she wanted it, it was fine with him.

Not that he was to blame for what had happened. The thing was, he hadn't had a hell of a lot of experience in these matters. He'd been with Cathy for so long, he no longer knew what was protocol and what was passé. Like opening the car door for a woman. He'd always done it for Cathy without thinking twice, but when he'd opened Rachel's door, she'd looked at him as if he *were* a dinosaur.

Maybe he had no idea of what to expect in the dating world, but one thing he was certain of—Rachel spelled trouble. Any fool could see that she was a woman with a secret, and fool was a role he had no intention of playing.

"You're so quiet," Erika said, her eyes on the road ahead. "I hope that what I said hasn't made you uncomfortable."

"No, you just took me by surprise." It wasn't the truth. Part of him had always suspected how Erika felt, even though she'd never made a move. Like he always said, a woman gave off signals. Still, he had chosen to ignore the signs, hoping the whole business would simply disappear. He knew he should have spoken to her long ago, nipped this fantasy of hers in the bud, but talking about feelings had always made him want to head for the hills. Cathy had known this, but it had never mattered. Even at the café on that long-ago New Year's Eve, when they had talked for hours about their plans for the future, she had understood his difficulty in expressing what he felt.

Not that he'd minded talking with Rachel. Not that he'd even known, at the time, that talking about feelings was precisely what he'd been doing. Which proved what he'd been thinking all along. The woman was wily.

Erika laughed. "Good. I'm glad you're surprised. All this time, I was afraid I was being too obvious. I didn't want to say anything until I felt you were ready."

Call him old-fashioned, but he wasn't used to a woman taking the initiative. Not that the idea repelled him. In fact, to his surprise he found it intriguing.

Was that perfume? An exotic blend of citrus and spices floated his way. Nice, he thought, although it wasn't the delicate fragrance that Rachel had worn, reminding him of roses. He pushed the memory aside.

He had to admit, Erika looked good. Her smoky-gray eyes were full of promise, her lips sensual in a rich shade of red. His gaze roamed over her bare shoulders, down to her clingy top, and he wondered if she was wearing a bra, one of those devices without straps. It had always mystified him how those contraptions stayed up, and right now he was itching to refresh his memory. His gaze dropped lower to her skirt, and he wondered what she would say if he reached across and rested his hand on her knee.

Somehow he doubted she would mind.

"Ready for what?" he asked playfully. "What exactly do you have planned?"

"First brunch, then a walk through Ballard Park. I don't want to rush you. I wouldn't want to shock you."

"Too late," he said, grinning. "I'm already shocked."

"Shocked, are you? Well, you'd better prepare yourself." She removed one hand from the steering wheel and placed it on his thigh. "The shock you're experiencing now is just a tremor compared to the earthquake I'm planning. After a romantic stroll, we'll get your car and head back to my place."

"Hey, both hands on the wheel," he teased.

"In case the world shakes?" She laughed again but removed her hand. "That's what I like about you, Adam. You're so cautious. You make a woman feel grounded." She flipped on the signal and turned onto Grove Road. "How does a champagne brunch sound? I've decided that you're taking me to that new Italian bistro in Ridgefield, just down the street from the Café St. Gabriel. It doesn't have a courtyard, but it *is* romantic. We can sit in the back, where it's private."

There was something about a woman in the driver's seat. Something about a woman at the controls. He leaned back and smiled, more than willing to go along for the ride.

When Rachel arrived to pick up Megan to take her to lunch, she was disappointed that Adam wasn't home. There was no denying it, she was attracted to him.

She'd spent a sleepless night, turning the issue over and over in her mind. Every time she'd pictured the way he'd driven those pucks hard against the boards, she'd broken out in a sweat. There was something about a man with drive that jangled her insides. Adam might be wounded, but he was strong. Strength of body, tenderness of heart. It was a lethal combination.

So why not pursue it? The answer was always the same: it would interfere with her plan. And it wouldn't last. Love, lust, she could call it anything she liked, but it always fizzled out. If she started something with Adam, what would happen when it ended? It would be like sleeping with the boss. After the affair was over, the employee always had to quit her job. Either that or she was fired.

If she were to pursue this, she *would* be sleeping with the boss. If it were just that, she could handle it. She could afford to take a chance with her job, but risking her relationship with her daughter was another story altogether.

There was also the issue of Adam's late wife. Rachel might be progressive, even liberal, but there was no way she'd allow three in their bed—even if one of them was only a ghost.

So. It was settled. There'd be none of *that*.

"Adam's at the auto shop," Paula said as Rachel waited for Megan to come downstairs. "Erika came by for him earlier."

Rachel berated herself. Adam had mentioned that his car would be ready this afternoon. She should have offered to take him to the garage. Driving with him alone in her car would have given her the opportunity to apologize for losing her temper last night, and apologize was what she intended to do. His continuing anger would only hinder her cause, and besides, she knew she had overreacted. He had every right to question her; after all, he was a father and she was spending time with his daughter. But after she apologized, she would make it clear—in a firm but gentle way—that there could be nothing between them. They would laugh about what had happened, and everything would be back on an even keel.

They would go on being friends.

Yeah, right. Friends. Who was she trying to convince?

She left with Megan and headed toward Ridgefield, planning to enjoy a quiet lunch at the Café St. Gabriel. It was a little pricey, but what the heck. It was her first meal out with her daughter. As she was parking the car, she thought she saw Erika and Adam farther up the street, coming out of another restaurant.

Once again, she chided herself for not offering to take him to the garage.

After a light meal of soup and salad, she and Megan shared a plate of rich French pastries. Later they stopped at a thrift shop and tried on old hats and coats, giggling at themselves in the mirror. The last stop was the fabric store, where they picked up a sewing kit. It was almost three when they finally arrived at Rachel's apartment, purchases in hand, eager to begin on the costume.

"You've made the apartment so pretty," Megan said, looking around the large room. "Uncle Steve will be so pleased with what you've done."

Rachel had hardly changed a thing. It wasn't as if she'd be staying here. As soon as summer ended, if everything went as planned, she'd be looking for a permanent place to live—a place with an extra bedroom for when Megan decided to stay over.

"All I did was switch the daybed with the bookcase,"

she said. The bed was now next to the French doors. "I like to feel the breeze at night."

"I know what you mean," Megan said. "Even in the winter, I sleep with the window wide open. I wrap myself in all my blankets. It makes me feel warm and snuggly."

Rachel knew exactly what she meant. That was the wonderful thing about their relationship. She always knew what her daughter was feeling. She believed she had always known, even during their years apart.

They spent the next hour converting an old black felt skirt and an embroidered white blouse into a costume. "This is exactly what Grace Farrel would wear," Megan said approvingly. She rose from the chair at the table and held the outfit against her. "What do you think?"

"It's perfect," Rachel said. "That is, it will be after I make some alterations. Why don't you try it on while I fix us a snack?"

Megan changed out of her clothes. From where Rachel stood at the kitchen counter, she could see the strawberry-shaped mark on her daughter's right shoulder. It was the same birthmark that Rachel's mother had, only Beth's was on her left shoulder. Rachel knew that birthmarks weren't necessarily related to heredity—they could arise during conception or pregnancy—but nevertheless, she saw it as further proof that she and Megan were related.

"That hat is wonderful," Rachel said, placing the tray onto the table. They had found a small beige cloche at the thrift shop on Main. A wide band embroidered with silver thread was stretched across the front, a large crepe bow tied at the back.

Megan giggled. "It's silly, isn't it? I can't believe people wore these things in the old days."

After Rachel had made a few adjustments to the waist of the skirt, she said, "There. Now the costume *is* perfect. Let's have that snack now."

"I should probably change before we eat." Megan headed toward the daybed, but stopped at the bookcase to pick up one of two small framed photographs.

Rachel's heart pounded. Had she remembered to put away the photos from the P.I.? She glanced over at her bureau. On top was the manila folder. She rose from the table and walked across the room. Discreetly, she opened the top drawer and dropped the envelope inside.

"Whose baby is this?" Megan asked, studying the photo.

"The woman pushing the stroller is my mother. I'm the baby."

For a moment Megan was quiet. "You look just like her," she said finally. She handed the photo to Rachel. "You and your mother must be very close."

"Actually, no. My mother moved to Los Angeles when I was nineteen. I haven't seen her since." Rachel hadn't seen her, but she had talked to her. She had just turned seventeen when she had run away, and a few weeks later, after finding out she was pregnant, she had called home. "We had a...falling out."

"You should call her. You obviously care about her, or you wouldn't have kept these pictures. You can't go through life waiting for the other person to make the first move. Before you know it, it could be too late."

Out of the mouths of babes, Rachel thought. "How did you get to be so wise?" she asked, amazed at her daughter's mature insight. But insightful or not, Megan's advice was something Rachel was not prepared to take. Her mother had always made her feel as though she were an inconvenience. It was Beth who hadn't wanted Rachel, not the other way around. If Beth wanted a reconciliation, she could darn well make the first move.

Rachel put down the picture, looking at the jagged line that ran across the glass in the frame. It was more than just a crack; it was a symbol of the deep divide that existed between the two of them.

Megan shrugged. "I'm not so smart. But my mom was. She always said never to put things off. She also said that life was too short for grudges." Her mouth quivered and her eyes filled with sudden tears.

"I'm sorry, Megan," Rachel said softly. "Talking about her upsets you."

"No, I have to talk about her. If I don't, I'm afraid I might forget her. Sometimes, even now, I have a hard time remembering what she looked like. Am I awful?"

She's fading, and I can't do anything about it. Adam had expressed the same concern to Rachel. "No, you're not awful, sweetheart. Time does that. It's only natural."

Megan sat down on the bed and stared out the widow. "Sometimes I wonder what she looks like," she said slowly. "My real mom, I mean. I'm adopted. Sometimes I wonder if I look like her."

"Do you think about her much?" Rachel asked, her pulse beating madly.

"I try not to, but I can't help myself. It's fine to say that life is too short to hold grudges, but I'm always asking myself why she gave me away. Dad says I shouldn't be concerned about someone who was never concerned about me, but I'm always asking myself what kind of person would give away her own child. She was probably a teenager without a husband, but it's not like it was in the old days. Nobody cares about those things anymore. Nobody cares if you're married or not."

"Maybe that had nothing to do with it," Rachel said

carefully. "Maybe your natural mother believed she was doing the best thing for her child."

"Like Erika wants to do the best thing for me? Send me away? You mean the best thing for *her*. People just can't go around getting rid of people! What about Grandma? How can sending Grandma to a nursing home be the best thing for her?"

"Maybe it's the only solution. At least she'd be able to get the care she needs."

"She gets all the care she needs at home. Paula is great, and Dad and I help out. Are you saying that Erika is right? Are you saying that when the going gets rough, we should all give up? What about my grandmother? Should she just give up and die?"

Megan was working herself into a frenzy. "I'm not saying that at all," Rachel said, reaching for her in an attempt to calm her. "I'm saying that sometimes we have to do things we don't like, because it's best for the other person. Like your natural mother, for instance. She probably knew she couldn't give you the kind of life she wanted you to have."

"Puh-leeze," Megan snorted. "In my book, you don't give people away like used clothes." She picked up the other photograph. "I didn't know you played the piano," she said, abruptly changing the subject.

For the first time since she'd devised her plan, Rachel was worried that Megan would reject her. She would have to tread carefully. Adam, it seemed, wasn't the only one with issues of abandonment. In his case his wife had died; in Megan's case, her mother.

"That's my mother again," Rachel said, forcing a smile to her lips. "She's the pianist in the family. Unfortunately I didn't inherit her musical ability."

"But you did! Only it wasn't the piano. Dad says you

used to perform in musical theater before you got a job as a teacher. You were a star!''

Rachel laughed. ''I wasn't a star. All I ever played were a few bit parts. I mentioned them in my résumé only to show that I've had some experience onstage, but most of my work has been backstage, helping and coaching young actors, much like I'm going to be doing at the community center.''

''You know what role I'd like to play?'' Megan asked.

''No, tell me.''

''Dorothy, in *The Wizard of Oz*. If I tell you something, you promise you won't think I'm being a baby?''

''No, sweetheart, of course not.''

''All Dorothy wants is to go home, back to Kansas. Remember when she says, 'There's no place like home'? Well, that's all I want, too. To stay at home, not go away. Except...''

''Except what?''

''Everything's changed. I wish things could be the way they used to be, before my mom died. But not even a wizard can change the past.''

Rachel looked at Megan's sad face. Growing up without a mother was not the life she had envisioned for her child. Twelve years ago, if she had known that this would happen, if she could have foreseen the future...

She knew she was being irrational. No one could predict the future. No one could have known that Megan would be left motherless.

The past might be as fixed as stone, she thought, but she would do everything in her power to make sure Megan remained right here, under her caring eye.

Something nagged at him as he and Erika entered the elevator in the apartment lobby. All through brunch they had bantered flirtatiously, but heading toward the park, he had begun to feel uncomfortable. Hollow. Something was missing.

When had he realized he was making a mistake?

It was when they were leaving the bistro. It was when he'd seen Rachel parking her car down the street from the café.

It was ironic, really. Rachel had believed she was a substitute for Cathy, when in fact he'd tried to make Erika a substitute for Rachel. Not that he was planning to do anything about his infatuation. He'd already decided that Rachel spelled trouble.

As planned, after brunch he and Erika had taken a leisurely stroll. Ballard Park, at the intersection of Gilbert and Main, had been alive with families picnicking in the lush grounds or simply enjoying the formal gardens. Erika had taken his hand and led him to the gazebo, which stood secluded among a mix of evergreen and deciduous bushes. "We're in luck," she'd said. "No one's inside."

Although the skies were clear, the air was still unseasonably cool. When he'd offered to run back to the car to get her jacket, she'd laughed and said, "I'm counting on you to keep me warm." Sitting next to her on the bench, he'd tried to tell her how he felt, but she'd been so happy, he hadn't had the heart.

Damn, he was a coward. He should have told her on the way to the park, when she'd suggested a weekend getaway to Cape Cod. He'd politely refused, using work as an excuse. God knew he could use some time off, but he was planning a few days with his family in Ocean City over the Fourth of July weekend.

He didn't want to hurt Erika, but he had to make it clear that they would remain just friends. He'd put it off long enough. And now he had another unpleasant task. He had to eat crow, to apologize for having led her on. And this was why he'd agreed to go back to her place.

After he'd picked up his car at the garage, they'd driven separately to her apartment. She'd pulled into the parking garage and he'd parked on the street. Now, riding with her in the elevator up to the third floor, he silently rehearsed his speech.

Feelings. He'd always been lousy at this sort of thing.

Erika turned the key in the lock and opened the door to her apartment. And gasped.

Adam pushed past her. "Wait here," he ordered. "They might still be in the apartment." In the living room, the floor was littered with books and magazines, which had been torn from their shelves and strewn everywhere. The television and CD player were intact, but the rack that had held her CDs was now empty.

"No, don't go inside!"

He didn't listen, and after a quick search of the apartment was back in the doorway. "It's safe. They're gone."

"My computer!" Erika cried and dashed into the den. A moment later she returned to the living room, a look of confusion on her face. "I don't understand. I have all this expensive equipment and all they took were CDs."

"It was probably that gang of kids," Adam said grimly. "What would they do with a stereo or computer? That kind of stuff is too big to carry out unnoticed, and where would they sell it?" He looked back at the door with speculation. "There's no sign of forced entry—they must have had a key. I'll call the police." He looked at Erika's face and paused. "What is it?"

"You can't call the police."

"Of course I'm going to call them." He reached for the phone and began to punch in the number.

She put her hand over his. "Think, Adam. What about Megan?"

"What about her?" He put down the receiver. "I can't believe you think that my daughter had something to do with this."

"It wouldn't be the first time she was involved. You're going to have to face facts, Adam. That girl needs discipline." She curled her lips into a tight smile. "There should be no doubt in your mind now. She has to go to the school in Manhattan."

"Actually, I've decided against it. I think she'd be better off at home, with me."

"Really."

There it was, that look of recrimination. Why was it that whenever he disagreed with her, he felt like an errant son? He thought of that song in *Annie*. What was it called? Right. "Little Girls." Every little girl was a mother in the making. From a very young age, they're given dolls to practice on, and then they grow up and practice on boys. Well, right now he had more than his share of females in his life. Lately it seemed that his mother, his mother's caregiver, Erika, Rachel and even his own daughter were doling out maternal advice.

"But Megan is such a talented girl," Erika protested. "You can't deny her this opportunity."

"She doesn't want to go, and I won't force her," he answered, his irritation increasing.

"How can she know what she wants? She's just a child! You're her father—you have to make these decisions for her. Up until last week, you agreed with me. Why have you changed your mind?" Her tone took on a chill. "Never mind, don't tell me. I already know. It's that woman, isn't it? I can't believe you'd allow a complete stranger to influence you."

"Don't be ridiculous. Rachel had nothing to do with my decision."

The look on Erika's face told him she didn't believe him. "Do you really know her, Adam? If I were you, I'd be a little more prudent about the people I allowed into my daughter's life." She gestured to the mess in her apartment. "Case in point. This is the handiwork of your daughter's so-called friends."

"Maybe those kids aren't responsible. Maybe this is the work of a professional."

"Who breaks into an apartment and takes only CDs? You said so yourself, it looks like the work of those kids. Mark my words, Megan was involved in this. She doesn't like me, and I can't think of a better way for her to let me know. She probably went through my purse, then sneaked out of the center to make a copy of my key."

"And when would she have done this?" he exploded. "During rehearsal, between the two acts in *Annie?*" He exhaled loudly. "Do you know what you're saying? You're saying that my daughter is a thief! She gave me her word that she's not involved with these break-ins, and I believe her."

"Her word? Listen to you! How can you take the word of that little conniver! Can't you see what's going on? I'm warning you, Adam, if you continue wearing those blinders, you're going to make things worse."

"For your information, Megan couldn't possibly have been involved in this. She's been with Rachel all afternoon. But I appreciate your vote of confidence," he added sarcastically.

"Rachel again," she said with scorn. "Talk about blinders."

"What's that supposed to mean?"

"That woman is after you and you're too blind to see. What's wrong with you, Adam? Open your eyes! She just arrived here on Thursday and already she's wormed herself in your life. Already she's playing Mommy to Megan. Let me tell you something, that woman smelled your money all the way from Hartford. Well, I have news for you. If you think I'm going to stand by and watch her reap what I've been sowing—" She paused. "I didn't mean that, Adam. I only meant—"

"Reap what you've been sowing?" Realization washed over him, leaving him with a sick feeling. "Oh, I understand what you meant, all right. I get the picture. No more blinders, remember?" He stormed toward the door. And stopped. On top of several papers scattered across the carpet was a shiny brochure. He picked it up. On the cover were the words *Belmont Manor*.

"Give that to me," Erika said, trying to grab the pamphlet from his hands.

He tightened his hold. "This is the name of that nursing home you've been talking about," he said in a low tone, trying to restrain his seething anger. He leafed through the booklet and pulled out a letter. He read through it quickly. "It says here that my mother is at the top of the waiting list. What have you done, Erika?"

"I only did what you didn't have the guts to do yourself," she retorted. "Your mother belongs in a home, and if you weren't so tied to her apron strings, you'd see the truth. All I did was get the ball rolling, call in a few favors. I didn't have to sign a thing. I just bent a few rules—it's not as if I broke any laws."

"Tell me something. When were you going to tell

me? What were you going to do when it came time to admit her? Forge a few checks?'' He turned his back and reached for the doorknob.

''Adam, wait!'' she implored, grabbing his arm. ''Maybe I shouldn't have done it without consulting you, but I was only trying to help. And about what I said before—all that gibberish about reaping and sowing—I know what you're thinking and you're wrong. I was jealous, and that's all. I've spent two years priming you for a comeback, and I won't allow another woman to benefit from my work. I won't lose you, Adam.''

He spun around. ''Priming me? Let me tell you something. I'm the only one who decides when I'm ready and when I'm not. And here's another news flash. When I'm ready, it sure as hell won't be with some control freak who's after my money. Lose me? Erika, you never had me.''

''You're making a big mistake,'' she said, her voice thick with desperation. ''Unlike someone we both know, I have only your best interest at heart.''

''My best interest or yours? What about my mother's best interest? What about Megan's? It seems to me you're a little too eager to ship her away, too. It's as if you want to get rid of every part of my life that's not connected to you. Besides the money, is there anything in my life you *do* like?''

Her eyes suddenly hardened, her desperation turned to spite. ''I thought you had potential, but apparently I was wrong. I don't have to take this crap. Get out. Go to your little tramp. You deserve each other. Maybe they'll name a soap opera after the two of you, *The Slut and the Sap*.''

He shook his head slowly. ''You were right. I *have* been wearing blinders. It seems I've been in the dark about a lot of things.'' He opened the door, and this time she didn't try to stop him from leaving. In the hallway, he turned to face her. ''As for the nursing home, if I could prove you did something illegal, I'd fire you on the spot, but knowing the way your mind works, I'm sure you've covered your tracks. I would suggest, however, that you think about resigning. I don't have legal grounds to dismiss you, but the community center is no place for someone with your lack of ethics.''

''Who are you to question my ethics? What gives you the right to judge me? You with your senile mother, your delinquent daughter and that tramp who calls herself a teacher! Well, I have news for you,'' she said, glowering at him. ''I have no intention of leaving. I know you, Adam. You'll change your mind about me. You'll realize I've been right about a lot of things.''

He was certain she was planning something—why else wouldn't she resign? He didn't know what schemes she was still entertaining, but if she thought he would change his mind, she was crazy. He headed toward the elevator, her anger like a blast of hot wind on his back. He might be forced to continue working with her, but he'd be damned if he spent another second listening to her raving.

He knew she was watching him, staring. Waiting to see if he'd really leave. In the past he'd always avoided confrontation, and she was probably thinking that he'd turn around and apologize, beg her to forgive him.

''Don't forget to call the police,'' he called, not looking back.

ACT TWO

Chapter Seven

Rachel was determined to talk to Adam, but he hadn't been home on Saturday when she'd dropped off Megan. On Monday morning she marched directly to his office, intending to have it out then and there. First she would apologize for her rudeness Friday evening and then they would go on as before—"before" meaning as if he'd never kissed her.

He wasn't in his office. Doreen told her that he had taken his mother for a routine checkup and that he wouldn't be in until later that day. Rachel resolved to talk to him as soon as he returned, but whenever she tried to corner him, he managed to evade her.

For the next few days, every time he ran into her in the corridor, or in the cafeteria, or in the parking lot, he'd mumble something about a meeting or a conference, then dash off. It was a strange way for an employer to act toward one of his staff, she thought, but lately,

strange phenomena and she were becoming good
friends. Every time she passed him in the corridor, or in
the cafeteria, or in the parking lot, her stomach tightened,
and every time he walked away her throat went dry.

As she sat at her desk reviewing costume and prop
lists, she tried to think of a strategy for improving his
attitude. Here it was already the first week in July and
he was no closer to thawing out than an Arctic iceberg.
Oh, he talked to her, but only when he had to—she did
work for him, after all—and his tone was crisp and busi-
nesslike, reminding her of when they'd first met. Unable
to concentrate on the paperwork, she leaned back in her
chair and thought about the coming Fourth of July.

Megan had told her that Adam was taking his family
and Paula to Ocean City for the long weekend. Knowing
that Rachel would be alone, Doreen had asked her to
accompany her to the parade in Middlewood. "I don't
want to go by myself," she'd said. "Even though Roger
is a bona fide veteran, he doesn't like to celebrate the
holiday. He hates crowds." Not looking forward to
spending the holiday alone, Rachel had readily agreed,
but now she was having second thoughts. She was in no
mood to celebrate. She tried to convince herself, to no
avail, that Adam had nothing to do with the way she
felt.

On the day of the parade, Rachel's mood still hadn't
lifted. But the sun was shining, the day bright and clear,
and she'd promised to meet Doreen at the fountain. She
stepped outdoors and was assaulted by a wave of hot,
muggy air, the sweltering heat aggravating her already
sour mood.

The annual parade was staged by the locals, and it
seemed that everyone from Middlewood had come out
to watch. Almost everyone, Rachel brooded, thinking of

Adam. The sidewalks were decorated with chalk murals, some showing Uncle Sam in his tall top hat, others depicting the American flag. Main Street was closed to traffic, allowing children to ride down the middle of the road, their bikes and tricycles decorated with streamers and balloons. Antique cars followed slowly behind, their costumed passengers throwing candy as bystanders scrambled to catch what they could.

"Looking for someone?" Doreen asked as Rachel scanned the crowd.

"I, uh, was just wondering how many people are here. It's a wonderful day for a parade. Maybe a little too hot, but it's better than all that rain we've been having."

"He's in Ocean City, remember? Even if he did change his plans, which I doubt, there are so many people here, you wouldn't find him in this crowd."

"I don't know what you're talking about."

"You know exactly what I'm talking about. In fact, everyone knows what I'm talking about, the way the two of you have been skirting around each other."

"That's ridiculous. You know how they love to gossip at the center. Have you heard what they've been saying about Erika? Diane Carter in accounting told Susan Peterson in sales that Erika and Adam—"

"Stop it," Doreen interrupted in a harsh voice. "I'm not interested in what any of them have to say. I'm only interested in Adam. I'm warning you, I won't let anyone hurt him again."

Rachel was taken aback by Doreen's sudden change in tone. Why would Doreen use the phrase "hurt him again"? She made it sound as if there had been more to Adam's relationship with Erika than he had let on. "I don't understand. Adam and Erika were just friends."

"I'm not talking about Erika. I'm talking about *you.*

It took him a long time to get over what happened to Cathy, and he's not done healing yet. He doesn't need any more pain. When he finds out who you are, it will be a shock. I won't let you toy with his emotions, on top of that.''

The ground beneath Rachel's feet seemed to shift, and she had to hold on to the lamppost to keep from falling. ''How did you know?'' she finally managed.

The blast of a trumpet sounded as a marching band approached. Doreen leaned forward and peered down the street. ''Here comes the veterans' float. It's always the first in the parade. It's a tribute to all our soldiers, but I'd like to think it's also a tribute to the wives. It wasn't easy for us, waiting back home, sometimes for months without a word. Evelyn, your mother and I pulled each other through a lot of tough times.'' She glanced back at Rachel. ''I knew you looked familiar the first time I saw you. Yes, Megan looks like you—I can see that clearly now that I know the truth—but the resemblance between you and your daughter wasn't what struck me. It was the likeness between you and your mother, except I didn't make the connection right away. It was your social security card that did it. It's in your maiden name, Cunningham. Then I remembered hearing something about Beth Cunnigham's teenage daughter getting pregnant and it all became clear.''

Rachel shook her head. ''Is there anyone in this county who *didn't* know my mother?''

Doreen smiled her answer. ''She was well liked, and so talented. Evelyn and I met her—heavens, when Adam was just a boy!—at Reverend Barnes's church in Ridgefield. After church the three of us had lunch, and before we knew it, we were meeting every day for coffee or just to talk. You might say we were a support group before that kind of thing became fashionable. With our husbands off in Vietnam, we had a lot in common.''

"Except my father didn't come back. I never even knew him. He was sent overseas when my mother was in her third month, and he was killed before I was born.''

"It was hard on your mother, but she made a life for herself. After she moved away, every now and then word came back about her success. Talent in the performing arts obviously runs in your family. How is Beth, by the way? It's been years since I spoke to her.''

"Me, too.'' Rachel stared blankly ahead, barely aware of the float rolling by. "Let's just say we don't get along.'' She threw her hands into the air. "Why on earth am I being so secretive? You might as well know everything, now that the worst part is out. Truth is, my mother and I never did get along. I was the proverbial teenager from hell. You know, sex, drugs, rock and roll. Looking back, I suppose it was my way of rebelling. Beth Cunningham wasn't the most attentive mother in the world. Not that I blame her for my behavior. I had all the answers, I was young and I was going to live forever. I had just turned seventeen when I ran away from home.''

"I think you do blame her,'' Doreen said. "You sound so bitter.''

"You bet I'm bitter, but not about the way she raised me. She probably did the best she could, and I can't fault her for that. But when I found out I was pregnant, she wouldn't take me back. Wouldn't let me come home. For that I'll never forgive her. There's nothing like unconditional love, is there?''

"I'm sorry, really I am. But it's all in the past.'' Doreen laid her hand on Rachel's, in a gesture of compassion. "Or is it? What about Megan's natural father?''

"He died young." Rachel felt a tear slide down her cheek. "The thing was, I really did love him. As wild as he was, I knew he loved me, too. I was sure we'd be together forever. I was wrong." She wiped away the moisture with the back of her hand. "So there you have it. I suppose you're going to tell Adam."

"No. You are."

Rachel swallowed hard. "I can't, Doreen. Not yet. I need more time."

"Time for what? It's obvious that Megan adores you, and I doubt that Adam will be sending Megan away to school, especially now that Erika is out of the picture. Don't you have what you came here for? Why do you need more time?" When Rachel didn't answer, Doreen's eyes became flat and lifeless, all compassion having drained away. "Oh. Is that why you came here?" she asked in a monotone. "Has his money sweetened the pot?"

"All I want is to be with my daughter," Rachel retorted, offended. "It's all I've ever wanted."

"Enough to marry Adam? If you played your cards right, you wouldn't even have to tell him who you are, risking his sending you away. You'd get to be a full-time mother to your daughter, and financially you'd be set for life. What a convenient arrangement."

"No, Doreen, no! The idea never even crossed my mind! You knew who I was right from the start—why are you accusing me of this now?"

"Because now the situation is different. Adam is walking around with his heart on his sleeve and I won't stand by and watch him get hurt."

"That's ridiculous," Rachel protested. "Adam is married to the past. He's not interested in me. All I want is to be with Megan, but I need some time to prove to him that I'm not a threat. I don't want to take Megan away from him, I just want to love her. Don't you understand? She needs me, and I would move heaven and earth for her.''

''Adam is like a son to me. I'd move heaven and earth for *him*.'' The expression on Doreen's face softened. ''All right. I don't like it, but I'll give you more time. I'll give you one month. The play goes on the first week in August. If you haven't told him by then, I will.''

The first week in August, Rachel repeated to herself. So much for having the whole summer to sway Adam and gain her daughter's love. To do this in such a short time, she just might have to move heaven and earth.

Erika was onstage, working with the cast, while Rachel sat in the third row of the auditorium, taking notes. The drone of Erika's voice was making Rachel drowsy, and she put down her notepad and closed her eyes.

Enough was enough.

Her problem, though, had nothing to do with Erika. It had nothing to do with the job, either. On the contrary, Rachel loved her work. The kids she taught were bright and talented, and they kept her on her toes.

She loved coaching, and as a result of her efforts— and Erika's, too, she grudgingly admitted—the play was coming along well. Paula had her own car, and with Evelyn in tow had begun to bring in Cinnamon, who had completely recovered, to rehearse with Alice Tucker, the girl who played Annie. Right from the start the cast had fallen in love with the puppy, adopting her as the center's mascot.

Megan was in both of Rachel's classes, musical theater and improvisation, and Rachel was grateful for every moment they spent together. For the most part her plan was working, and she and Megan were growing closer. It was what she had dreamed of, what she wanted.

There was, however, an obstacle. It was the second week in July, and Adam was still behaving as though she had the plague. His attitude was rattling her nerves and was something, she decided, that needed correction. Immediately. Because of the plan, she told herself. She needed him as an ally, not a foe.

But it was more than just her nerves that were rattled, she admitted, remembering the way he had kissed her— the first time with so much zeal he'd winded her, the second time with so much tenderness she'd thought she'd dissolve.

From upstage, Erika's voice broke into her thoughts. "Rachel! Pay attention!"

Rachel picked up her notepad, but it was hopeless. She couldn't concentrate. She felt Adam's presence as if he were right there in the theater, watching her, studying her. She felt a prickling at the back of her neck and turned her head.

He *was* there, sitting in the back row as though he were in hiding.

Enough was enough.

With newfound resolution and an impulsive burst of courage, she made her way to the back of the auditorium. No time like the present, she thought, sitting down beside him. She searched her brain for an opening line. "Megan is terrific, isn't she?" Rachel asked, pleased with herself. Children were wonderful icebreakers.

"She's perfect for the part of Grace," he answered, looking straight ahead. "I guess Erika was right, after all."

Was that *remorse* in his tone? She was eager to know

what had happened between him and Erika. Rumors were flying that he'd been the one to cool their relationship—a relationship that, according to the center's gossipmongers, had been a hot topic for months. The way he was looking upstage now, his gaze in Erika's direction, made Rachel wonder if he was regretting his decision.

"Even Cinny is perfect," she said. As soon as the words were out, she wished she could take them back. Erika had been against casting Cinnamon in the role of Sandy. Wouldn't Adam regard what Rachel had said as a cheap shot?

He turned his head and smiled, dispelling her worry. "Paula has been so helpful, offering to take the puppy back and forth to rehearsals. In fact, I'm glad you and Megan convinced me to put Cinnamon in the play. It's led to a lot more good than anyone could have foreseen. The first time Paula came to the center, my mother ran into some old friends. She remembered every one of them. She even remembered their children's names."

Thank heavens Evelyn didn't see me, Rachel thought. What if being around these old friends had triggered another memory? Thinking that Rachel was a much younger Beth, Evelyn might have asked her about her life in Hartford. "How do you like living in the city?" Rachel imagined the older woman saying. "And how is your new baby? I heard you named her Rachel."

"These friends of hers asked her to join them in their next water aerobics class," Adam continued. "When Paula told me how alert my mother had been, how excited she was about doing the aerobics class, I felt like kicking myself. Why hadn't I thought of it myself? I know all the classes here—I arranged most of them. So I enrolled my mother, and she seems to be benefiting. I really believe she's making progress. Since she started the program, she hasn't once tried to run off, and her temperament has definitely improved. Not only that, the classes give Paula a break.'' He chuckled. ''Right now Paula is in the gym. Something about cellulite.''

''Do you think leaving your mother here is wise? The center isn't equipped to handle Alzheimer's patients. What if she has a seizure?''

''You sound like Paula. I had a hard time convincing her, too. My mother is on medication now, so the likelihood of her having a seizure is small. Besides, this class was designed for the over-sixty crowd. The staff is well trained. And my mother's condition is hardly what you'd call advanced. She's only in the early stages of the disease.''

Rachel opened her mouth to speak, then changed her mind. It was obvious that Adam was in denial. ''I'm glad everything is working out,'' she said uneasily. She knew that nothing she could say would convince him that his mother was not getting better.

There was another reason she didn't speak up. She knew she was being selfish, but for the first time in what seemed like forever, he was talking to her. Not just barking out some request related to the job, but actually talking. For the first time in days he didn't seem tense or distracted, and she didn't want to spoil the mood.

This was the best possible time for an apology. ''About the things I said—''

He silenced her with a touch to her lips. ''Forget about it. I said some pretty nasty things myself. Everyone has a few secrets, and I had no right to pry.'' He flashed her one of his disarming grins. ''I figure you'll tell me sooner or later, when you're good and ready.''

He had that all wrong. She would tell him when *he*

was good and ready. And he obviously wasn't. As long as he saw only what he wanted to see, he'd never see her side of it. If he couldn't accept his mother's situation, how could Rachel expect him to accept hers?

All this was academic, she thought gloomily. August was coming up fast. If Rachel didn't tell him, Doreen would.

Adam leaned in closer, his leg brushing against hers. "What do you say we start over? How do you do, Ms. Hartwell. I'm Adam Wessler, your obnoxious, arrogant boss."

She laughed, remembering that first day in his office when he'd used those same words. "Seems to me you're always asking for another chance," she said jokingly. "Okay, we'll start over—again."

She looked at his face. Merriment shone from his steel-blue eyes, and deep in that laughter was warmth and sincerity. "I'm glad we're talking again, Adam," she added with honest affection. "I'd hate to think we couldn't be friends." With a shock, she realized just how true those words were. Their friendship had come to mean more to her than just a tool to help her get close to Megan. It had taken on a life of its own, something completely apart from the plan.

"Friends?" he repeated. "Who are we kidding? I've turned this thing over and over in my mind. This so-called friendship has been keeping me from doing my job. Keeping me awake at night. During the day, I find myself staring out the window, my mind a million miles away. At night I lie in bed, tossing and turning, and let me tell you, it's not my mind that keeps me awake. I tried to ignore it—tried to ignore you—but it's like a nagging itch that doesn't seem to want to quit. And don't try to tell me you don't feel the same way. Every time

I run into you, I see that look on your face, that look in your eyes.'' He cupped her chin with his hand, tilting her head upward. ''That look is still there.''

Here they were again, back to that same old thing. Why couldn't a man and a woman just be friends, without all those hormones?

She met his eyes, intending to protest, but what she saw arrested her. Reflected back to her was her own desire. A need she'd buried long ago, it was now, against all resolve, awakening.

She was aware of his other arm around the back of her seat, aware of a current pulling them together as though they were magnets. Darn it, he was right. The way she felt had nothing to do with friendship. He moved his arm onto her shoulder and drew her closer, sending a surge of heat racing through her veins. This time, in the back row of the theater, in the dimness that sheathed them, this time if he lowered his head to kiss her, she knew there would be no turning back.

''Adam! Where are you?'' shrilled a high-pitched voice from the stage. ''Adam, are you out there? They're trying to drown me! Adam, where are you?''

''What now?'' he muttered. He jumped out of his seat and rushed up the aisle, Rachel following closely behind. Evelyn stood by the stage door, soaking wet in her bathing suit. Downstage the cast of *Annie* stood watching as the strange scene unfolded before their eyes.

''You must be freezing,'' Adam chided, taking off his jacket. ''Here, Mom, put this on.''

''I'm fine,'' Evelyn answered, jerking away. ''I don't want you to ruin a perfectly good sports jacket. What would Cathy say?''

''I don't want you to catch cold. Stick out your arms.''

Evelyn spun around to Rachel. ''You're Beth Cunningham, aren't you? I heard your husband was sent overseas. You shouldn't be alone, especially in your condition. My, my, you hardly show at all!''

"Can we please get back to rehearsal?" Erika shouted at the cast. "In case you've forgotten, we have a show to put on."

Megan shot her a cold glance, then turned to her grandmother. "Grandma, what's the matter? Don't you remember Rachel?"

"Crazy old biddy," Erika mumbled, and left the stage.

Rachel glanced around. As far as she could tell, no one else had heard the cruel remark, and she was grateful. A comment like this would have caused Megan and Adam unnecessary pain.

The aerobics instructor burst into the theater. "Here she is, thank God. I turned my head for just one second, and she was gone. I'm so sorry, Adam. I never realized this could happen."

"You never realized this could happen?" he echoed. "You deal with seniors all day and you never realized this could happen?"

"I treat the body, not the mind," the instructor answered huffily.

Adam looked over at Rachel, his face wrenched with guilt. She knew he was thinking about what she'd said only moments ago, about the center being ill equipped to handle Alzheimer's patients. Her heart went out to him. She hated to see him berating himself, and she hated to see him in so much pain. Evelyn was getting worse. It had to be torture watching a parent deteriorate.

"Apparently we need to review the entire senior program," he said. "I'm sorry, Carol. This wasn't your fault. Will you take my mother to the locker room?"

Somewhat mollified, the instructor answered, "No problem. I'll wait with her until Paula gets back. My assistant is with the class. Come, Evelyn, I'll help you change back into your clothes."

Evelyn's mouth was set in a stubborn straight line. "I am *not* going with her."

"I'll do it, Grandma," Megan piped up. "I'll help you get changed."

"Get away from me, you little monster! You're with *them*."

Megan turned pale and looked at Rachel. "What did I say?" she said, her voice breaking. "What did I do?"

"You didn't do anything, sweetheart," Rachel answered. "It's not your grandmother's fault, either. It's the disease… Megan, wait!"

But Megan had already backed away and was running down the aisle.

Rachel laid her head against his back. She could hear the wind whipping against his jacket, but she wasn't concerned. She was warm. Protected. His body was her shield. Nothing could harm her when she rode with Colton, sitting behind him, holding on to his waist.

The dream shifted to the night of the accident. He'd been swerving in and out of traffic and had skidded on an oily patch of road. Even though they'd hit the truck head-on, she'd emerged from the accident without a scratch. As though it had happened yesterday, she saw herself riding with him in the ambulance, holding his hand.

"Don't leave me," she saw herself pleading, but he couldn't hear her, couldn't see her. The fight in him was gone. She closed his eyes with her fingers.

Like wildfire, strands of his red hair splayed across

her hands. She touched his face, feeling the warmth of his flesh grow cold beneath her fingers. She realized it wasn't his flesh that was turning to ice; it was her own.

They told her that Colton might have lived if he'd been wearing a helmet. Might have lived to see his child. She felt the baby stir in her womb, jarring her out of her shock.

As in a play, the scene in the dream changed, and she saw Megan running down a dimly lit street. She saw Megan's face contorted with fear, Megan's wild red hair flying in the wind. Then, suddenly, Megan was gone. Rachel looked down every alley, around every corner, but she couldn't find her.

She heard a soft, mournful cry. *No louder than a whisper, as plaintive as a song on the wind.* Although the voice was muffled, as when Colton would call out to her from the front of his bike, the meaning was clear: Megan was in trouble.

The sudden ringing brought Rachel back to the real world, waking her up with a start. She scrambled out of bed and reached for the phone on the bureau. Unlike the voice in her dreams, Adam's was loud and clear. The message, however, was the same: Megan needed her.

Rachel glanced at the alarm clock next to the phone. It was almost two. Something had to be terribly wrong for Adam to call her at this hour. "I'm on my way," she said.

On the short drive over, she thought about what had happened during improv class that afternoon at the center. The rules of the exercise had been simple. Working in pairs, one student was to be the slave, the other the master. The servant had to act out everything the master said to do, as long as it wasn't in bad taste. The point of the game, Rachel explained, was to build up self-control. Each child would have a turn at being the slave and the master, and after the game ended, they would talk about how they felt. The incident occurred when Megan was the slave. When her partner told her to break into the king's castle and steal his gold, Megan had shouted that the game was stupid and childish, and refused to play it any longer. "A king's castle," she'd said derisively. "What are we, five years old?" She'd retreated to a corner and sat down, hugging her knees to her chest.

At the time Rachel had believed that Megan was reacting to what had happened earlier on the stage, but the more she thought about it, the more she became convinced that something else was bothering her, as well. Even in a game, the idea of stealing had upset her.

At Adam's house, Rachel found her sobbing into her pillow. She calmed her down, and after Megan had dozed off, Rachel sat on the edge of the bed, stroking her hair, listening to the gentle cadence of her breathing. It was several minutes before she went back downstairs.

"She's asleep," she said, finding Adam in the kitchen.

Adam jumped up from his chair. "What did she say?" he asked, his face riddled with concern. "My mother I can handle, but when it comes to Megan, I don't have a clue. It seems that my daughter took another one of her nocturnal prowls. She came home hysterical, but she wouldn't tell me where she went or what happened. I'm sorry if I woke you, but these days you're the only adult she listens to. So what's my next step? Put a padlock on her door? Put iron bars on her window?"

Rachel sat down, motioning for him to do the same. "Megan was upset because of the incident on the stage.

Your mother called her a monster. This was what set her off.''

"You don't have to be a psychologist to figure *that* out. I was hoping you'd be able to learn where she went tonight.''

Rachel sighed. "She told me she went to the park across from city hall. That's where they usually meet. Sometimes they meet at a friend's house, when the parents are out.''

"What about the break-ins?" he pressed on. "Did she mention them?''

"She swears she had nothing to do with them. Only…''

"Only what? What else did she tell you?''

"It's nothing she said. It's the way she looked.'' Rachel's thoughts returned to the improv class. "She's scared, Adam, and she's afraid to tell us why. Your mother's behavior might have set her off, but something else is going on.''

"So you're saying she *is* involved in the robberies. It seems that Erika was right, after all. Megan is out of control. I *have* been wearing blinders.''

Just hearing that woman's name made Rachel's blood churn. "Megan is not a thief,'' she answered in a clipped tone. "She's a good kid, Adam. Have a little faith in her. Erika was right about those blinders, but that's all she was right about. If you remove them, you'll see that your daughter couldn't possibly be involved.''

"Blinders,'' he repeated with obvious self-contempt. "A nice euphemism for ineptitude.''

"You're not inept,'' she said. "For what it's worth, I think you're doing a great job as a father, in spite of the problems. It's not easy being a single parent, and you have a lot on your plate.''

"I wasn't just talking about Megan. Look what happened at the center today. I sure missed that one, all right. The aerobics instructor hit the nail on the head when she said, 'I treat the body, not the mind.' The program focuses on the physical only. None of the senior programs touch on any other issues associated with aging. If something had happened to my mother, I would have been responsible. If something had happened to anyone else, the lawsuits would already be piling up on my desk. I see now that even someone in the early stages of Alzheimer's needs special attention. Someone like my mother. She's basically all right, but she needs that little extra care. I provide it for her at home, and I should be able to provide it for her, and others like her, at the center."

Adam still refused to acknowledge that Evelyn was far beyond the early stages. The incident today might have opened his eyes to the needs of seniors in principle, but as far as his mother was concerned, to borrow Erika's phrase, he was still wearing blinders.

"Adam, about those blinders—"

"Yeah, I know," he said, frowning. "You keep trying to get it through my dense brain that you're not interested in anything other than friendship, but I just keep charging in. Even now, in the middle of all my family crises, I feel like reaching over and taking you in my arms, pulling you closer, kissing you again.... I'm sorry, Rachel. There I go again."

The conversation was making her dizzy. In just a flicker of time, he'd gone from his daughter, to his mother, to kissing Rachel. "I'm not talking about—"

"You were right all along," he continued. "We can't go this route. For whatever reasons, you've made up your mind that you don't want a relationship, and as for me, you can see for yourself that my life's a mess. At least we can stay friends. You know, platonic. Let's just blame it on bad timing and leave it at that.'' His face grew solemn, his eyes wistful. ''Maybe you should go away and come back in a year. Maybe by then we'll have our acts together. As for now, it's too bad that all this electricity, all this energy, has to go to waste. Between the two of us, we could open a power plant.''

If she thought she was dizzy before, now the room was spinning. Only a short time ago he'd been talking about staring out of windows, about tossing and turning in bed. After the speech he'd delivered in the auditorium, now he wanted platonic? What happened to that itch that wouldn't quit? Did he run out after work and pick up some calamine lotion?

He wasn't an emotional yo-yo; he was a perpetual boomerang.

At the front door he gave her a quick peck on the cheek, then thanked her again for being there for Megan. ''That's what friends are for,'' she said, feeling somewhat let down.

Friends. Wasn't this what she wanted?

As she drove home, an idea—a ridiculous, absurd, insane idea—began to take hold in her mind. In truth, it had been simmering since the Fourth of July, when Doreen had accused her of it, only now it was crystallizing into something real.

Friends made good spouses. The bottom line was, if you couldn't be friends with the person you were married to, it would be like sleeping with the enemy. Adam was an honest, caring man. She could do a lot worse in a partner. She could be content as his wife, and she would be living with her daughter.

No. Never. Absolutely not.

She turned onto her street. Darn. Someone had taken her parking spot. Because her neighbors seemed to come and go only at night, she was convinced they were vampires. It was the only explanation she could think of. It wasn't any crazier than the idea buzzing around in her head.

Marrying Adam to become Megan's full-time mother was preposterous. Out of the question. Marrying him and not telling him who she was would be even crazier. As if she could keep the secret locked away. Even if she could wipe out all the records to her past, Doreen had made it clear that she would tell Adam if Rachel didn't.

And what about love? Rachel already knew the answer. Love wasn't real. It was just a dream. People married for love all the time, and half those marriages ended in divorce. Who was to say that a marriage based on respect and friendship wouldn't have a better chance of survival?

Yet Adam believed in that dream. He had lived the dream with Cathy, and as much as he tried to fight it, he was headed there with Rachel. When a man acted the way he did, it was a sure sign that he'd been hit with Cupid's arrow. But because of his devotion to Cathy, Rachel knew that he wasn't the type of man who took love lightly. When he did fall in love again, he'd want to go the full nine yards. Which meant marriage.

Rachel also sensed that for him love and sex were intertwined. If he'd been interested in casual sex, he and Erika wouldn't have been just friends. For him, making love meant being in love.

"Adam is walking around with his heart on his sleeve," Doreen had said. Even though he was advocating friendship, Rachel was sure that all he needed was a little push. After that, it would be smooth sailing. She knew she would have to tell him who she was—she had until the first week of August or Doreen would do it for her—but wouldn't he regard the truth as a bonus? Not only would he be marrying the woman he loved, he would be marrying the mother of his child.

His child—*her* child—was the only reason she was considering the idea.

A car was pulling out across the street from her apartment. She waited for it to leave, then parallel parked into the tight spot. She smiled to herself, but the smile had nothing to do with her parking skills.

Maybe the idea wasn't so preposterous.

And face it, even though she didn't love him, she had to admit there was something about him that turned her knees to jelly. For her the marriage would be one of convenience, but who said that the sex had to be a duty?

Chapter Eight

It was time to put the new, improved plan into action, and it was a plan she had to execute as flawlessly as a triple axel. Too much was at stake.

The next day she finished work early and headed to the arena. She sat on the bench, watching the Zamboni move back and forth across the rink. Adam wasn't expecting her to show up at this time, and he certainly wasn't expecting what she had in mind. What if he rejected her?

Her pulse quickened as anxiety gave way to anticipation. What if he didn't?

She glanced at the clock over the doorway to the arena. It was almost five. Adam would be here any minute.

During the day, ice time was divided between public skating, group classes and private lessons; the evenings were reserved for hockey. During the lunch hour and from five to six the rink was reserved for staff use, but so far, she and Adam were the only ones who took advantage of the arrangement. Adam usually skated right after work and Rachel preferred to skate at noon. Like him, she enjoyed the solitude. Not having to worry about colliding into another skater, she could concentrate on her jumps and spins. Still, she would have liked to skate with her daughter, but Megan claimed she didn't like the ice. "It's not the fall that hurts, it's the sudden stop," she'd said.

To Rachel, skating was more than just a sport; it was an art. When she was on the ice, all her problems seemed to melt away as she glided across the smooth surface. Every line and angle of the body worked together to create the illusion of perfection, but unlike art, the emotion spent in the process could not be described in words or paint.

After the Zamboni had disappeared into its cavelike home behind the rink, she removed the guards from the blades of her skates and stepped out onto the ice. She always skated her best after the surface had been cleaned. The holes and cracks were filled in, the slush cleared away. The indentations made by previous skaters had been wiped away like footsteps in the sand.

With arched back and bent knees she pushed off with her left foot and glided forward. She repeated the motion with her right foot, stroking across the ice. Left, right, one foot crossing over the other, gracefully, rhythmically, she moved around the arena.

There he was, right on schedule.

Through the clear Plexiglas above the sideboards, she could make out the back of Adam's head as he headed into the bleachers. She'd know that proud gait anywhere. It's funny how quickly a person's impressions can change, she mused. In just a short time, *arrogant* had become *confident*. She'd also believed him to be a stickler for convention. Hardly. He seemed to make the statement, "I answer to no one."

He sat down to change into his skates, then looked up and waved at her, causing her pulse to jump in her throat. Face it, she thought. She liked a man who thought well of himself. She found his confidence to be downright sexy.

He was downright sexy.

He jumped off the wooden bench. This was her cue. She skated to the other side of the rink and fiddled with the sound system behind the gate. Filling the arena with its haunting tones, the musical track for "Memory" from the Broadway play *Cats* spilled into the chilly air. Alluding to happy times gone by, the lyrics played in her head as she skated back to the center ring.

Maybe this song wasn't such a good choice. Adam didn't need to be reminded of old memories. But the music was so hauntingly beautiful, so alluring, how could anyone resist its enticement? She tossed her worry aside.

She pretended not to watch him as he hopped onto the ice and skated toward her, sweeping a puck with his hockey stick. To her surprise, he passed her without even a nod of his head and disappeared through the gate from which she had just emerged. A moment later both he and Rossini's "William Tell Overture" erupted onto the rink.

Twisting his body around, he dug both blades into the ice, then came to a stop just inches from where she stood, spraying her with shavings of ice.

"Thanks," she said. "I needed a shower."

He grinned. "What's the matter? My kind of skating too rough for you?"

"You call that skating?" she teased. "I call it mangling the ice. So where's your apple, William?"

He looked confused. When he didn't answer, she explained, "The apple you're planning to shoot off my head. Or in your case, hook with your hockey stick. William Tell was a Swiss patriot in the fourteenth century. When he refused to salute an Austrian governor, he was ordered to shoot an arrow through an apple on his son's head."

"Thanks for the history lesson, but I prefer to think of myself as the Lone Ranger. Don't you watch reruns? This music was the theme song for the TV show. With his faithful Indian companion, Tonto, the daring Lone Ranger fought for law and order in the early West. At the end of every show, he mounted his fiery horse, Silver, and rode off into the sunset."

"Thanks for the lesson in TV memorabilia, but just the same, keep your stick away from my body." She felt her face turn scarlet. "I, uh, mean—"

Ignoring her comment, he saluted her and took off across the rink. "Hi-yo, Silver!" he called, not looking back.

Stupid, stupid, stupid. How could she have said that? She stood there, berating herself as she watched him dribble the puck. It was as if he were maneuvering a slalom course, weaving in and out through invisible cones. His concentration was unwavering as he strove to keep the puck in the center of the blade.

Maybe he hadn't heard what she'd said. It was obvious that the only thing on his mind was hockey.

What was it about men and their toys? Hockey sticks or horses, the toys were basically the same. Well, there was more than one way to separate a cowboy from his horse, and one of those ways was to give him a challenge. She skated back to the gate, and a moment later the song "My Funny Valentine" wafted through the air.

She glanced at him sideways. Just as she'd planned, the change of music had caught his attention. "Like I said," she called out to him, "you call that skating? Get a load of this, hotshot." She planted her feet firmly on the ice and twisted vigorously by rotating her arms and legs counterclockwise. It was a rudimentary two-foot spin, one she had done countless times in the past, but when Rossini's overture suddenly sliced into the air again, she was caught off guard and lost her balance, landing flat on her rump.

"Having problems?" he asked, coming to a quick stop behind her, once again showering her with ice.

She scrambled to her feet. "If you think it's so easy, let's see you do it."

"Is that a dare? What do I get if I do?"

"If you complete the spin—and that means you have to do at least three full rotations—you get to listen to your music. If you don't, I get to be the D.J."

"I'm already listening to my music. You'll have to change the stakes."

"Just what do you have in mind?" she asked boldly. Okay, so maybe her remark about his stick had been a little much, but who said they couldn't engage in some good old-fashioned flirtation?

He raised an eyebrow. "I can see how this could get interesting. Okay, how's this? If I fall, you get me as a dancing partner. We put on your music and we skate your style."

"If you fall, what good are you to me as a dancing partner? I want someone with a little finesse."

"You'd be surprised at how gentle I can stroke," he said without missing a beat.

And she'd thought *her* remark was racy? "Okay, hotshot, what happens if you don't fall?" she asked, feeling her cheeks reddening again.

"We play hockey."

"Let me get this straight. If I win, I get to risk breaking my leg by dancing with you. If you win, I get to risk breaking my leg by playing hockey. What do *you* risk?"

"I come here every day at this time to shoot pucks. I'm willing to risk losing my practice time. I'd say I'm being very generous."

She didn't have much choice in the matter, she thought as she watched him prepare for his spin with a series of backward crossovers. He leaped into the air from a left-foot takeoff, and after completing a full revolution in the air, landed on his right foot and spun around several times, his left leg extended straight behind.

She stared at him, momentarily speechless. He had just completed a flying camel spin. "I feel as though I've been hustled," she reprimanded. "You've been holding out on me. What else can you do?"

"I aim to show you," he answered smoothly.

"I was referring to your skating skills, hotshot."

"I can't do much without toe picks, but I won't need them for what I have planned."

"And just what is it you have planned?" she bantered.

"Hockey, lady. Wait right here and I'll get you a stick."

He was serious about playing hockey, and here she'd thought he'd been flirting. She groaned. Good grief, hockey?

A moment later he came through the gate, carrying another stick. "We keep extras in the storeroom in case one of the PeeWees breaks one. Here, try this. Just your size."

Scowling, she grabbed the stick. "If you think I'm going to play this stupid game without a helmet, you're mistaken."

He rolled his eyes. "Wait right here." He darted away and quickly returned with a helmet. "This should fit. Another PeeWee accessory. Sorry if it doesn't go with your outfit."

She was surprised he'd noticed what she was wearing. She suspected that if a Hollywood sex symbol showed up wearing only her goose bumps at an NHL game, not one man would even turn his head.

"What's wrong with my outfit?" Her leggings and long-sleeved top were stretched skintight across her body, allowing for freer movement but chosen to accentuate her every curve. Maybe he needed glasses.

He eyed her critically. "How come you're not wearing one of those little tutus? I like it when a skater moves forward, her leg sticking straight out in back, into the air. That little skirt just flips right up. Cute, very cute."

"Tutus are for ballerinas, not figure skaters, but if we ever do get to ice dance together, I'll take your preference under advisement." His eyesight was just fine, she thought, miffed. "By the way, where's *your* helmet?"

"Hey, I went and got you one, but there's no rule that says I have to wear one, too."

"I am not participating in this ridiculous, dangerous endeavor unless you wear a helmet."

Once again he skated away. "Satisfied?" he asked a few moments later, back at her side. Patterned with stars and stripes, his headgear was similar to hers.

She followed him to the center of the rink. "Judging from our helmets, I suppose this is where you tell me you play hockey for the good of the nation."

"You got that right," he said, dropping the puck. "If we held a hockey match every time we felt the urge to go to war, think of how many lives would be saved. Now pay attention. That's your net—" he motioned across the rink "—and the other one is mine. Don't go shooting the puck into your own territory. That's my job."

"I may not like the game, but that doesn't mean I don't know how to play."

"Now don't get sensitive on me. If you want to play a man's game, you have to act like a man."

"There are female leagues, in case you've forgotten." She narrowed her eyes. "You're skating on thin ice, hotshot. On one hand you want to see all female skaters in tutus, but on the other hand you want them to be like men. Make up your mind."

He sighed. "Look, are we going to play this game or not?"

"Do I have a choice?"

"Now you're learning. Okay, listen up. Normally we have to wait until the referee drops the puck to start the face-off, but since there's no referee, I'll count to three. Then we each make an attempt for the puck."

"Why do you get to count? I think that under the circumstances, I should get to count. Since you obviously think I can't play, I should be given a handicap, which means I should do the initiating."

"Why are we discussing handicaps? This isn't golf. Besides, I thought you *were* initiating."

Ignoring him, she moved her hand down the stick and

fixed her eyes on the puck. "Ready? One...two..." She scooped the puck and began sweeping it down the ice.

"Hey!" he shouted, scrambling after her. "You jumped the gun!" In a second he was beside her, checking her with his body.

"You'd better keep out of my way or I'll have to give you a penalty." She pushed him off and extended her stick in an attempt to keep him at bay.

"Body checking is legal. What you're doing is not. It's called high-sticking." The puck slid by his feet. When he scooped it and started racing away, she tried to restrain him with the blade of her stick. "And that's called hooking," he said. "Very illegal."

The puck slid in between them, and both sticks began their battle for control. A duel on ice, she mused, lifting her sword and reverting to her high-sticking stratagem. He stepped back and she took off toward the net. Just as she was setting up for a shot, he skated up behind her, dropping his stick and grabbing her around the waist.

"I believe that's called holding." She squirmed free of his hold and spun around. "For that I get a penalty shot."

"This has to be the wackiest game I've ever played. You're making up the rules as we go along."

"What's the matter, hotshot? Too tough for you? Now stand back while I take my shot." She skated toward the goal posts and stopped less than two yards away.

"You're too far from the net," he called out from behind her, laughing.

"You think?" She moved in closer. "How's this?" A thought occurred to her. "What do I get if I make this goal?" she asked, turning around to face him.

"You get to make me dinner."

"What happens if I don't make this goal?"

"You get to make me dinner."

She smiled inwardly. Little did he know, he had just stacked the odds in her favor. Getting him to her apartment would bring her one step closer to the payoff.

She moved the puck to the heel of her stick and positioned the blade. She drew the stick away from her body while sliding her hand lower down the shaft. As she was about to slam the puck forward, Adam once again reached for her from behind, foiling her maneuver. In an instant the two of them were flat on the ice, his body on top of hers.

She looked up at him, for a moment stunned. Then she flashed him what she hoped was her sexiest smile, intending to take full advantage of the situation. An opportunity like this—completely accidental yet tailored toward the cause—might never knock again. In this case, however, *knock down* was a more apt description.

"Are you okay?" he asked, concern in his voice. "You have a strange look on your face. Are you in pain? I didn't mean to trip you. I just wanted to stop you from shooting."

"I've taken worse falls than this." So much for opportunity, she thought, slightly affronted. A strange look? He thought her sexy smile was strange? Either he was made of stone or the fall had knocked him senseless. Either way, he wasn't making any attempt to detach his body from hers. "Are *you* all right?" she asked.

"I haven't been all right since the day you walked into my office. I think I've fallen pretty hard. Isn't it obvious?"

What was obvious, pressing hard against her stomach, was the part of him that *did* seem made of stone. In spite of the ice beneath her, she felt her body heating up. It was like sitting by a campfire on a winter night, your backside freezing, the front of you burning.

Suddenly she was nervous. Here she was lying on her back with him on top, when at any moment Doreen or Megan—good Lord, her own daughter!—could come prancing in. "Uh, Adam? I think we should get up."

His eyes shone with an intriguing mix of lust and merriment. "I have you in a position where you can't run off and you want me to let you go? I think I like keeping you in one place, all to myself. Besides, this is the closest I've ever come to an old fantasy of mine. Haven't you ever wondered what it would be like to make love stark naked in the snow?"

No, she could honestly say she hadn't. She couldn't believe she was lying under him, on the ice, listening to him go on about his fantasies. Not that she wasn't willing to try something, well, different. She was just as adventurous as the next person, but a warm, comfortable mattress seemed a lot more practical than a bed of snow.

Then again, there was something erotic about his suggestion, strange as it was. And there was definitely something erotic about the way she was lying beneath him, out in the open as if the rink were their personal winter wonderland.

His steel-blue eyes bored into her. The temperature in the arena was below freezing, but it wasn't the air that caused her to shiver.

"Just how cold would it have to be?"

"I wouldn't worry about that," he said, his voice husky. "You and I generate so much heat, we could make toast. I can already feel the ice starting to melt."

Whoa. Was he talking fantasy or did he actually think they would make love *here?* This was a public arena in Connecticut, not a snowfield on their own private glacier. And even if they were the only people in the whole continent, no one could possibly keep up with the exhausting tempo of the ''William Tell Overture''—which he had somehow rigged to play on continuous repeat.

He scrambled off her and extended his hand to help her up. ''Game's over,'' he said brusquely. ''You win. That is, you would have won if I hadn't tackled you. Of course, we were playing by your rules.... What is it, Rachel? You have that strange look on your face again.''

She dusted the frost from her leggings, feeling more than a little foolish. Maybe he hadn't been contemplating acting out his winter fantasy right here on the ice, but why had he turned off so abruptly? The human boomerang soars again, she thought. Well, she was tired of it. It was time to take action. She drew in a nervous breath. ''Adam Wessler, are you going to kiss me or not?''

''Not that I mind playing by your rules,'' he answered breezily, ''but I can't kiss you.''

''Then I'll just have to kiss *you*.'' She leaned in closer and pulled his head to hers, but the only thing that connected, with a loud clunk, were the stars and stripes of their helmets.

''Interference,'' he said innocently. ''Another infraction that merits a penalty.'' After removing his gloves, he took off his helmet and put it onto the ice. Slowly, agonizingly, he undid the straps beneath her chin as if he were undressing her. Finally he removed her helmet and placed it next to his.

There was no longer any interference as he pulled her toward him, crushing her into his chest. At first his kiss was slow and drugging, his tongue languidly exploring the recesses of her mouth, and then it became insistent, probing, his mouth coveting hers with unrestrained hunger.

If this was his idea of a penalty, she couldn't wait for the reward.

"By the way, I usually eat dinner at seven," he said hoarsely, his lips making their way down the side of her neck. "A bet's a bet."

"There might not be time for dinner," she murmured back. "I have to defrost the refrigerator—" she paused for a long moment while he revisited her lips "—and I'll need some help throwing all that cold snow out onto the floor." She looked up at him, trying to match the innocent look he had given her only moments ago.

His face broke into a knavish grin. "As I recall, my friend Steve has a self-defrosting refrigerator, not one of those slush-amassing relics. So where snow is concerned, I guess we'll have to wing it. Unfortunately—" he brushed her forehead with a light kiss "—it'll have to be some other time. Tonight we're having dinner at my house. Paula has the evening off, and you're cooking for me and Megan."

"And here I thought we were playing by *my* rules."

"I never doubted it," he said teasingly, stuffing the puck into the pocket of his sweatshirt. Carrying both helmets by their straps with one hand, the two hockey sticks with the other, he skated off. At the gate he raised the sticks in a hi-yo-Silver salute.

After dinner she had helped Evelyn with her bath, then settled her in for the night. Now, sitting at the foot of Megan's bed, she listened as her daughter rehearsed her lines.

I could get used to this, she thought with contentment.

It was what she had missed growing up. Family life. A sense of belonging.

"So what do you think?" Megan asked after pausing for a break.

"I think you've got the character down pat. You're a natural."

"Really? You don't think I sound dumb? I've always played kids' roles. I have to admit, I thought it would be a lot harder playing a grown-up, but it's easier than I thought."

"That's because you're no longer a kid. You're a young woman." And she was, Rachel thought sadly, not for the first time regretting the years she'd missed with her daughter.

"As long as I don't sound like a little kid trying to act older," Megan said. "But I guess the costume will fix that. I mean, it'll make me look older, don't you think?" Her face lit up. "And I have just the thing to finish it off." She jumped off the bed and pulled out a small velvet box from the top drawer of her dresser. "Here," she said, handing it to Rachel. "Open it." She sat back down on the bed, looking at Rachel expectantly.

Rachel snapped open the top. A heart-shaped pendant, studded with tiny diamonds, hung from a delicate gold chain. Something nagged at the back of her mind. There was something familiar about this necklace, something vaguely disturbing. "It's beautiful, Megan. Where did you get it?"

"It was my mother's. Dad bought it for her for their fifteenth anniversary, but she never got to wear it." When Rachel didn't respond, Megan said, "You're probably thinking it makes me sad. It doesn't, not anymore. What makes me sad is that it's being wasted, stuck away in a drawer. Dad says I'm too young to wear diamonds.'' She fingered the locket she wore around her neck. ''I know I said I'd never take this off, but I think I should wear the pendant in the play. It's perfect for Grace. Annie is the one who wears a locket. Not *my* locket, of course.''

Rachel carefully lifted the necklace from the box. And then she remembered. It was the necklace she had seen in the dressing room on the night of the opening. The necklace she had *imagined* seeing, she quickly amended.

She stared at the pendant, transfixed. ''Maybe wearing it in the play isn't such a good idea,'' she said, her voice sounding tinny in her ears. ''It looks expensive. What if you lose it?''

''I don't lose things. I'm not a kid anymore—you even said so yourself. I want to wear my mother's pendant and I don't see why I can't. Rachel, are you listening to me?''

Rachel looked up with a start, as if she'd suddenly awakened from a dream. ''It's not up to me, Megan. You'll have to ask your father.''

''Forget it,'' Megan said, snatching the pendant out of Rachel's hand. ''He'll only say the same old thing. I'm too young, blah-blah-blah. I don't want you to talk to him, either. He'll only give me another lecture and I'm sick of them. I'm sick of everyone telling me what to do.''

''Megan—''

Without warning, tears began to rain down Megan's cheeks. Clutching the pendant, she slumped down on the mattress and buried her face in her pillow.

Rachel reached over to stroke her daughter's hair. ''You miss your mother,'' she said, putting aside her confusion about the necklace.

''You don't understand.'' Megan's voice was muffled

against the pillow, and Rachel had to strain to hear. "Sure I miss her, but that's not what's bothering me. I don't even know what's wrong. I didn't mean to snap at you, but sometimes I can't stop myself. I yell at Dad and Paula all the time, even Grandma. What's the matter with me?"

"What you're going through is normal. It's called puberty, remember?"

Megan sat up and wiped away her tears. "Yeah, I know, hormones. Either I'm really happy or I'm miserable. Tell me something, will it ever get better?"

"Not really," Rachel answered, trying to alleviate the mood with humor, "but I promise you that when you're older, it will get interesting." A lot older, she fervently hoped, remembering some of the overly developed girls she'd taught in Hartford.

"You mean sex."

Rachel laughed. "I guess I do."

Megan forced a weak smile. "That's what I like about you. You don't talk to me like I'm a little girl, the way Dad does." After a slight pause she asked, "If I tell you something, will you promise not to tell him? If he knew, he'd look at me funny and start acting weird."

"I can't promise that," Rachel said honestly.

To Rachel's surprise, Megan giggled. "Oh, never mind. He'd figure it out eventually, anyway. He already knows I wear a bra." She smiled shyly. "I got my first period. I have it now."

Rachel smiled warmly. This was one of those once-in-a-lifetime moments, meant to be shared by a mother and daughter. "It's now official. You're a woman. Do you have everything you need, or should we make a trip to the drugstore?"

"Paula bought me a box of pads months ago so I'd

be ready. I'm wearing one now, but it's so uncomfortable. One of my friends at the center gave me a tampon, but I was too embarrassed to ask her how it works. Do you think you could show me? Not show me, exactly. Kind of talk me through it.''

Well, I wanted quality time, Rachel thought a few moments later as she stood outside the bathroom door, calmly giving instructions. The door was open a few inches so that Megan could hear, but out of respect for her daughter's privacy, Rachel made sure to stay out of view.

Quality time? No question about it. Were they bonding? Without a doubt. To Rachel, bonding meant getting personal, and it didn't get more personal than this.

Adam's father had practiced law with eloquence, but at home he'd habitually resorted to crudeness. ''Don't think with the wrong head,'' he used to tell Adam. ''It always leads to trouble.'' Frank Wessler might have been crude, but what he'd said was true—and one thing Adam didn't need was trouble.

I am my father's son, Adam thought with self-recrimination as he sat in the living room, waiting for Rachel. He couldn't believe the things he'd said to her at the rink. *Stark naked in the snow? How gentle I can stroke?* She had to think he was some kind of pervert. Kinky. Definitely weird.

Not that she seemed to have minded. Which baffled him. Had he missed something? Sometime between last night and this afternoon she'd changed her mind about their relationship. When exactly had this happened?

When it had happened was irrelevant. Last night they'd agreed to remain friends, and he still believed it was the best way to go.

He'd remind her of this as soon as she came back downstairs.

He glanced at his watch. It was after nine. She'd been upstairs for more than an hour. What in heaven's name was taking so long? She was supposed to be helping his mother with her bath, not giving her swimming lessons.

He had something to say, and the sooner he got it over with, the better.

She'd arrived at six-thirty, looking adorable in a tank top and shorts, her rich dark hair still wet from a shower. "Put me to work," she'd said. "I aim to please."

He'd wanted to tell her right then and there, but instead he'd found himself saying, "You make the salad and prepare the potatoes. I'll take care of the heavy stuff, like tending the grill. I don't want to wear you out."

"And why is that? Do you have something vigorous planned for later? Like another hockey match?" She'd turned to him with that strange look on her face, and added, "Maybe we should order a pizza. Barbecuing is a tough job. I wouldn't want to wear *you* out."

"It's not hockey I have in mind." And then he'd kissed her. Hard and forthright, giving the word *vigorous* a new definition.

Nervously he rose from the couch and began pacing. He had to get his act together. Had to start thinking with the head on his shoulders. But damn, she'd looked good in those skintight pants today on the rink. How did women get into those things? It was as if she'd been wearing nothing at all, her skin like a canvas that had been painted in jade. Lying on top of her on the ice, he'd easily imagined what she would feel like naked under his touch, her full breasts pressing against his chest, her long willowy legs twined around his waist…

Stop it. Now. Tell her before it gets out of control.

He headed out of the living room.

"All's well upstairs," she said, meeting him in the hallway, flashing him a dazzling smile. "Your mother is fast asleep and Megan is studying her lines.... Adam, what's the matter? You have a strange look on your face."

No, *good* was the wrong word to describe how she'd looked on the ice, and it was the wrong word for how she looked tonight. If her shorts were any shorter, her tank top any tighter, they would be downright illegal.

Thankfully, he wasn't a cop.

Not answering, he swept her into his arms and continued where they'd left off in the kitchen.

Chapter Nine

Rachel was humming as she cut out paper snowflakes. Fold the paper in two across the diagonal, then again, and once more, snip out a pattern along the edges and open it up. She attached the cutout to a string, and after clambering to the top of the bureau, taped her creation next to the other snowflakes already hanging from the beam in the ceiling.

Next on her list was snow. Over the past few days she'd taken home boxes of paper that had been shredded for recycling. What a stroke of genius, she praised herself, dumping box after box over the bed and onto the floor. Shredded white paper made great snow. The most creative snow, however, had come from the center's art studio. Blues and greens and reds intermingled with the white, creating an ambiance of celebration. Wasn't what she was planning a kind of celebration? A mating ritual, she thought, feeling a flush of anticipation.

She looked around the room. Something was missing. What could she add to make the apartment even more festive? Then it hit her—Christmas. Christmas in July. From a large poster board she cut out a tree, then decorated it with colored markers.

She stood back and looked at the tree now taped to the wall. It still wasn't enough. Elves, she thought with a burst of inspiration. She'd make little elves in bright-green pants and pointed red hats and tape them to the wall.

Or maybe not. They'd be like voyeurs. She wanted to excite Adam, not inhibit him. Then again, any man who would pin her to the ice and confess his most secret fantasy probably wouldn't blush easily.

It was thumbs-up for the elves.

That done, she folded the empty boxes and stashed them in the closet with the art supplies. She retrieved two tennis balls and put them next to the phone. Next to the counter she built two pyramids, using empty soda cans.

One last job and the stage would be set. She crossed the room and set the air conditioner to max. It wouldn't take long for the room to become a freezer. Well, not exactly a freezer, but Adam would get the idea.

She felt like a teenager again. She couldn't count the number of furtive glances they'd exchanged, the number of secret kisses they'd stolen over the past week. Not to mention the touching in his office, backstage at her desk, in the kitchen at his house when they were sure no one was looking. Ever since she'd lost the bet out on the rink, they'd had dinner together every night, usually at his house with his family and Paula. Occasionally they'd eaten at one of the restaurants in Middlewood or at one of the trendy cafés in Ridgefield. But never at her place.

It was never just the two of them. She'd suggested more than a few times that he come over, but he'd declined, saying he knew where it would lead.

Wasn't that the point?

She supposed it was a good sign he wanted to go slowly. As old-fashioned as it was, it meant he was serious about her. He wanted to be sure, and wanting to be sure meant only one thing—he had something permanent in mind.

But time was running short. She had two weeks left to tell him who she was, or Doreen would do it for her. But before Rachel could let the cat out of the bag, she had to make certain she had the cat *in* the bag, in a manner of speaking.

Enough of his I-want-us-to-get-it-on-but-I-can't attitude! If it took a fantasy to make a reality, a fantasy he would get.

Too bad I don't own a tutu, she thought giddily as she changed out of her skirt and jersey. Not that he would balk at what she'd chosen for the occasion. She'd picked up a thigh-length blue fun-fur jacket at the thrift shop—*campy* would be the word to describe it—and a silky azure scarf with ruffles on the end. Aside from these two pieces, she was planning to wear only a smile.

After dinner at his house, she'd told him she had to leave early to work on an art project. It was the truth. Her paper creations could attest to that. She glanced at the clock on the bureau. Nine-thirty. It was time to put her plan into action. By now Evelyn would be in bed, and Megan would be in her room, rehearsing her lines.

Rachel punched in the number. After only one ring Adam picked up the phone. "I called to hear your voice," she said. "I miss you already." That was also the truth; she'd just left him a short while ago, and already she ached to see him. They chatted a few more minutes, and then she said, "Hold on a minute, I thought I heard a noise." She crossed her fingers behind her back; this was where the fiction started. She counted to thirty. "It was nothing. No, wait! There it is again." She held the receiver motionless and this time counted to twenty.

"Rachel, are you there?" she heard through the receiver. "What's going on?"

She didn't answer.

"Rachel, are you all right?"

"I'm fine," she said finally, pretending to be out of breath. "I looked outside, but I didn't see anything. Probably just kids and their pranks. They're gone now." After all the break-ins in the neighborhood, she knew that the mention of "kids and their pranks" would set off warning bells in his head. And now for the clincher. She picked up a tennis ball and threw it at one of the pyramids. And shrieked.

"What was that? Rachel? Rachel! I'm coming over. Get out of the apartment, now!"

"I told you, it's nothing," she said, picking up the second tennis ball. Crash. "Adam? Are you there?" But he'd already hung up.

All those drama classes were paying off in a way she had never imagined. Now all she had to do was clear away the jumble of cans from the floor and wait for nature to take over. In less than a minute she had shoved the cans into the recycling bin, and just as she had predicted, less than five minutes later the doorbell rang.

Excitement gave way to misgiving. What if he laughed at her? She looked at the elves on the wall and felt her stomach drop. They were childish. No, not childish. They were just plain stupid.

This was a mistake. She was making a mistake.

Now he was pounding on the door. She glanced at the elves again and groaned. She opened the door a few inches, leaving the chain in place. A blast of hot air blew into the cold apartment, but it wasn't the heat that set her cheeks on fire.

On the landing stood two police officers.

A rosy-cheeked young man who didn't look old enough to shave flashed his badge through the crack. "I'm Officer Connors, and this is my partner, Officer Reynolds. We got a call about a possible prowler. Mind if we take a look around?"

A tall, shapely blonde nodded at her. When Rachel didn't answer, the woman said, "Ma'am? May we come in?"

"Uh, this isn't a good time for me. Maybe you could come back tomorrow?"

She knew her response made no sense. If she didn't let them in, there would probably be a SWAT team outside her front door in minutes. She removed the chain and opened the door, stepping aside to allow them to enter. With one hand she pulled the fur jacket close to her body, trying to make sure it didn't open in front— not an easy task, considering that it had no buttons or snaps. With her other hand she tried, without success, to tug it lower down her exposed thighs.

Connors eyed at her suspiciously. "We'll just take a quick look, ma'am. It'll only take a minute."

Take a quick look, indeed! The way he was ogling her, you'd think he'd never seen a woman in a fur jacket. Okay, it was the middle of summer, the fur was bright blue, and all she had to do was bend an inch in any direction for him to see clear to Kansas.

"I'm sorry, Officers. There seems to have been a mistake.'' There'd been a mistake, all right. Adam had called the police. Stupid, stupid, stupid. Not him, her. She should have anticipated his reaction. He was a thoughtful, responsible person, which was one of the reasons she was so drawn to him. ''I thought I heard someone in the yard, but it was only—'' she heard a raucous noise almost like a quacking, as if outside someone was trying to start a motorbike ''—ducks.'' Good Lord, ducks? ''I, uh, mean cats. The neighborhood is full of them. Cats everywhere.''

''Cats,'' the leggy blonde echoed, looking at her strangely. She stuck her head inside the bathroom just as Adam came bursting in through the door.

''Rachel!'' he called out. ''Are you all right?'' He rushed past the police and halted, staring at her curiously.

''I'm fine,'' she said, tugging at the fur. ''I don't understand why everyone is making such a big deal. I heard a noise, but it was nothing.''

''Ducks,'' Connors said.

''Cats,'' Reynolds corrected. She turned to Adam. ''Are you Wessler? The guy who called?''

''Yeah, it was me. Sorry.'' He winked at Rachel. ''Apparently it was a false alarm.''

''No problem, sir,'' Reynolds said. ''You did the right thing. These days, with so many cats and ducks running amok, a person can't be too careful.'' She looked back at Rachel. ''You'd be surprised at what runs around loose. Hey, bug-eyes,'' she said to her partner, ''let's go.''

''You might want to get that air conditioner looked at,'' Connors said, heading back to the door. ''It's awfully cold in here. You don't want to overload the wiring and start a fire. Oh, there's one other thing.''

"Yes?" Rachel asked, anxious for them to leave. The sooner they left, the sooner she could get to work giving her dignity a proper funeral.

"Merry Christmas, ma'am."

The two officers laughed as they headed down the stairs. "Did you get a look at those snowflakes?" Rachel heard Reynolds ask. "And what about *her?* Talk about flakes!"

"Ho, ho, ho!" Connors said, laughing. "Say Reynolds, I have an idea. Why don't we go back to your place and start the holiday season ourselves?"

Reynolds punched Connors playfully on the shoulder, and they disappeared around the bend of the staircase.

Rachel closed the door, afraid to turn around. She'd never live this down. It wouldn't be long before Middlewood's entire police department would be engaging in Santa's-little-helper jokes. She didn't even want to think about what must be going through Adam's mind.

She turned around, expecting the worst. He walked over to her, smiling mischievously.

Was he laughing at her? She averted her eyes.

"Look at me, Rachel." He gently pulled her hands away from the front of her jacket.

"I can't. I feel like such an idiot…. Adam, what are you doing?" He pushed the jacket open and slid it off her shoulders. "Oh" was all she said as it hit the floor.

"You're so beautiful. Do you know how long I've been thinking about this? I must have been out of my mind to wait. Do you know how long you've been driving me crazy? Talk about crazy—crazy and wonderful— I can't believe you did this. A fantasy tailored just for me. For us. Only it's not fantasy. It's happening. It's really happening."

It was freezing in the apartment with the air on max,

but it wasn't the cold that was tingling her nipples. Here she was wearing only a scarf, facing him, while he stood fully clothed, drinking her up with his eyes. Never before had she felt so naked, so exposed. She felt as if hundreds of tiny feathers were massaging her skin.

Desire had overcome embarrassment, and she reached for him in an attempt to remove his shirt. He pushed her hands away. "Not yet," he said, cupping her breasts with his warm hands. "Indulge me. This is another fantasy of mine."

"To make love with a woman while you're still dressed? Isn't that, uh, anatomically impossible?"

"Not just any woman. This fantasy is just for you. And right now, making love *to* you, not *with* you, is what I have in mind." He outlined the circle of her breasts, and she let out a shudder. "I've been thinking about this since the first day you stepped into my office," he continued, smiling at her devilishly. "Every time you crossed and uncrossed your legs, I thought I would lose control. I kept thinking about what it would be like to have you sit naked on that hard chair across from my desk while I conducted the interview."

"Tell me about the position, Mr. Wessler," she said without batting an eyelash.

"For starters, Ms. Hartwell, there's the matter of the dress code." With a light tug on the ruffles, he ran the scarf down between her breasts, across the flatness of her belly. He wrapped it around her back, and then roughly, almost violently, pulled her against him.

The scarf fell to the floor.

Through his clothing she could feel the extent of his desire. Tilting back her head, he kissed her, thrusting his tongue deep into her mouth. Making her want to pull him right in. Making her want to devour him completely. Once again she grabbed at his shirt.

"Not yet," he said a second time.

He pulled away, lowering his hands between their two bodies, his fingers weaving a slow, erotic path across her belly. Fingers searching, feeling their way, he seared a path down her abdomen, lower still. Involuntarily, she parted her legs. She was a flower, his hands the sun. She blossomed under his touch.

He entered her with one finger, and then with another. He flicked his fingers inside, and she gasped with delight. Up and up, as if on a roller coaster slowly climbing to the peak of the world, she soared, begging for the release that only the drop would deliver.

"Now," she moaned. "Now."

Oblivious to her command, he moved his mouth down to the flesh of her belly. She was climbing higher still, to that place where nothing else mattered. She climbed up and up, higher and higher on her sensual roller coaster, as slowly, languidly, he lowered his mouth.

She hadn't counted on his turning her inside out, exposing her insides as easily as he had exposed her flesh. She hadn't counted on feeling this way.

She was sure it was all over her, how she felt. She was sure he could see it written all over her skin. There was no hiding from his steel-blue eyes. No hiding from his hands or his fingers. No hiding from his tongue, which had joined his fingers in his quest to drive her over the edge.

He didn't have to try very hard.

She was overtaken by a series of riveting shivers, and for a moment the room seemed to spin. She opened her eyes, momentarily lost, then breathed in deeply as though she had been under the water too long and had only now come up for air.

"You're hired, Ms. Hartwell," he said teasingly. "How do you like the benefits so far?"

This was the man she'd had to coerce? This was the man she'd believed needed persuasion? She laughed, and it was with joy.

She wanted him again. This time, completely. She raised her hands to his chest, and this time he didn't push her away when she grabbed at his shirt. Frenzy took over as their four hands fumbled to remove his clothes. He ripped off his shirt as she undid his belt. He kicked off his shoes and she slid his trousers down his legs. A moment later he was standing before her, as naked as she was.

He was magnificent. Could such a word be used to describe a man? His shoulders were massive, his legs long and muscular. And wondrously proportioned, she thought, coveting him from his head to his toes. She let her gaze linger on his groin, the word *modest* no longer part of her dictionary.

He locked his hands on her spine and pulled her against him. She leaned back, arching instinctively. And then straightened up. "Adam, wait," she said, breathless. "We need to…I bought some…"

A look of confusion crossed his face, and then he smiled shyly. "Don't laugh, but I've only been with one partner my whole life. You have nothing to worry about."

She returned his smile. "I won't laugh at you if you don't laugh at me. I haven't been with anyone since my marriage."

"I'm told it's like riding a bike. You never forget."

"Just the same, we should be careful. You wouldn't want to get me pregnant."

"Not right away," he said, and her heart did a sudden flip-flop.

She scooted over to the bureau. "What's your pleasure, sir? I picked up an assortment. I never realized these things came in different flavors! Even black cherry, my favorite flavor of soda. It's your favorite, too, right?" As she spoke, she realized her mistake. His favorite soft drink had been one of those little tidbits the P.I. had included in the report.

"Who told you I was a pushover for black cherry?" Adam asked, laughing. Before she could answer, he said, "Sorry, bad guess. I like orange."

Looks like my eloquent P.I. goofed again, Rachel thought, remembering how he'd omitted that small detail about Adam's inheritance. If it hadn't been for the resemblance between her and Megan—a resemblance that thankfully only she and Doreen were aware of—she might have started doubting that Megan was even her daughter.

No, she'd recognize her daughter no matter what she looked like.

As Rachel closed the bureau drawer, her thoughts hurled back to the present moment. Adam had approached her from behind and was curling his hands around her breasts. A dizzying current raced through her. His chest was still pressed against her back as he lowered his hand, and she could feel him sliding on the condom. With one quick motion he pushed inside her, and she gasped, grabbing the top of the bureau to steady herself.

He doesn't waste any time, she thought. There was nothing gentle about the way he had plunged into her, nothing gentle in the way he was kneading her breasts, the way he was moving inside her. And she liked it. She liked what he was doing. She wanted him deeper, harder, and she made her desire known.

Was that me? she thought, amazed when she called out. Was that my voice? It was as if she were outside her own body, looking in. Her back remained molded into his chest, his hands on her breasts and everywhere at once. He increased the momentum, one forceful thrust after the other, and she was inside her skin again, lost in that dim space between reality and trance. She was drifting away, further into her own self, yet she was aware of every inch of him as he continued to move.

Something seemed to open inside her, and she could feel it opening in him, too. She wasn't sure if he had called out her name, or if she had spoken his. For a brief span of time they were one and the same person, one trembling body glistening with sweat.

When their breathing had returned to normal, he turned her around and wrapped her in his embrace. Without warning, a tiredness came over her. Just when she thought her knees would collapse, he scooped her into his arms and laid her down on the bed.

"Now that we got that out of the way," he said playfully, "we can get down to the real business."

Although he was joking, there was something wistful in his eyes, something that told her he was nearing a place that scared him. But it was a place he would go to, with her, if she let him. He caressed the side of her face with so much tenderness, she thought she would cry.

It wasn't fatigue she was feeling. It was the last of her resolve draining away.

She couldn't bear it, and excused herself to go to the

bathroom. She looked in the mirror. Is that me? she thought, suddenly angry with herself. Angry that she had allowed herself to forget the reason she had set out to seduce him. Angry that she had allowed herself to feel with more than just her body.

Her palms were sweaty, her forehead clammy. She turned on the water, hoping to wash away this feeling of relinquishment. She had to pull herself together. She couldn't lose sight of the goal.

"Rachel," he said moments later, as she approached the bed. "I love the sound of your name."

He pulled her down next to him and moved his hands gently over her breasts. She felt herself melting, her anger dissolving, and in an instant she was there again, in that space where there was no separation between body and spirit. She reached down, returning his caress.

She felt him growing again, in her hands. "Don't you need time?" she asked. "I thought it took at least a few minutes between, uh, sessions."

"I guess I forgot to read the rule book," he said, brushing his lips along her neck. "Now that the initial commotion is over, we can take our time to get to know each other properly." He moved his lips in a wavy path across her belly, slowly down one leg, all the way to her ankle. Then moving to her other leg, he worked his way back up along the inside of her thigh, until he had reached his destination.

This time when she felt the familiar quivering, she was fully aware of her surroundings. She was lying in her bed, atop a makeshift snowbank, moonlight streaming in through the French doors.

She sighed a woman's contentment.

"Don't move." He hopped out of bed and picked up the package of condoms from the top of the bureau.

"You did say you bought a whole assortment, didn't you?" He slipped back in the bed, next to her. "I certainly hope so. There are only three to a package."

She laughed, and he rolled on top of her. She felt him again, only it wasn't his tongue that was demanding her attention. Hard and insistent, he entered her, but this time he went slowly, teasing her with his unhurried pace and filling her up completely.

She closed her eyes. She didn't want to look at him.

"Rachel," he said softly. "Open your eyes."

"I can't."

"I don't want to hurt you, ever. Am I hurting you?"

"No," she whimpered. "Yes."

"Do you want me to stop?"

"Yes…no."

It was his tenderness that was hurting her, killing her. She wanted it rough, the way it had been the first time. Maybe it would jar her back to reality. Keep her from slipping away.

But he wouldn't quicken his pace and she was sure she would disappear. Lose herself completely. Again she was climbing, as if she were on that roller coaster. But this time she knew there was no going back. No going back to the person she had been.

She felt her climax growing. Faster, she wanted to cry out, but she couldn't speak, couldn't breathe.

We're water now, she thought. Clear, pure and sparkling. His breathing changed and finally he increased his tempo, the paper snow on the bed crunching under their bodies as they moved together, quickly, in perfect rhythm, rushing to their release. This time when they crested, he looked right into her.

She realized, with relief, that she hadn't disappeared. She was right there, in his eyes.

* * *

Adam lifted his head and glanced at the clock on the bureau. It was almost two. Rachel was snuggled close to his body, her back curled into his chest. He tightened his arms around her and felt her stir.

"Mmm," she murmured. "I like waking up knowing you're here." She twisted around and looked at him. "I should be angry at you. You've been holding out on me."

"You ain't seen nothin' yet. The night is still young."

She laughed. "You're a man of surprises," she said, tracing little circles on his chest. "As a matter of fact, you've been holding out on a lot of things."

"Like what?" he asked, lazily enjoying her touch.

"For instance, hotshot, your skating skills. Why didn't you tell me you could figure skate?"

He leaned on his elbow, careful not to let her hand fall away. "I was born with blades on my feet. My mother used to skate."

"Evelyn was a skater? You're kidding!"

"Why would I joke about something like that? In fact, she was serious about it. She even went all the way to Nationals. She was once a very different person," he added quietly.

"Before the Alzheimer's," Rachel stated.

"No, I mean when she was younger. A lot younger. I have wonderful memories of a young, vibrant woman. I guess, over time, living with my father changed her. Oh, he was never abusive, not physically. He was just a cold, stern man with a loud temper. But she loved him. Worshiped the ground he walked on."

"You sound bitter."

"Bitter? Yeah, I'm bitter. Take skating, for example. I got hooked really young. My mother started taking me to the rink when I was only three. She was willing to go the whole route with me, training, coaches, long hours on the ice, but my father called it a sport for sissies. Squashed that dream like an insect. I started playing hockey, and that was okay with him. More than okay. He considered it an Ivy League sport. That was another thing that put a thorn in his side."

"What do you mean? You just said he'd been okay with hockey."

Rachel looked so earnest, Adam had to stop and plant a kiss on her forehead. "What I mean is that I chose Berkeley over Harvard, which pissed him off royally. He thought Berkeley was too radical. He wanted his son—and future partner in the firm—to be a Harvard graduate."

"And when you didn't go to law school, he was angry," Rachel said. "You chose to follow your own dreams. Now you're the director of the community center. You listened to your heart and you're successful. If he were alive, he would be proud."

"Would he? I'm not so sure. Yeah, I'm bitter, but I'm also regretful. Not for the decisions I made about my career, though. I was happy teaching, but after so many years, I felt it was time to move on. What I regret is that I never made the effort to make my father understand. He was a hardheaded old mule, and I gave up. Walked away. When I made the decision to go to school in California, he made it clear that I was a disappointment. I barely spoke to him after that."

She snuggled closer, putting her head on his chest. "I know how you feel, but there's nothing you can do about it now. You should let it go."

"Just because he was a lousy father didn't mean I had to be a lousy son," he continued as though she hadn't spoken. "I could have gotten through to him. We could have reconciled. Now it's too late."

Without speaking, she reached up and touched the side of his face.

She'd done it again. Got him to spill his guts. What was it about her? It must be her eyes, he concluded. Hypnotic. Magic. They had cast a spell over him that first day when she'd waltzed into his office. "Enough of the past," he said. "I'm starving, woman. Feed me."

She laughed. "It's the middle of the night and you want breakfast?"

"I wasn't talking about food."

She leaned over him and studied him with those green, bewitching eyes, her smooth, ivory breasts brushing against his chest. He pulled her down, into the circle of his arms.

Adam was asleep, one arm draped across her waist. She slipped out of bed and tiptoed to the closet to get her robe, then stepped out onto the narrow balcony.

The night was star-filled, reminding her of their first kiss at the center's opening. The air was clear with just a scent of dew. Soon dawn would be breaking and another glorious day would begin. She inhaled deeply, the wonder of life filling her lungs, moving right through to her soul.

She'd been convinced she would never feel like this again. For years she'd felt like a wooden puppet, going through the motions of living. She thought back to her marriage. She'd met her husband at a ski resort. She'd just come in from the slopes, and he was sitting in the lounge, his leg in a cast. Her feeling sorry for him led to their dating and eventual marriage. She'd believed she loved him, but something had been missing, and until Adam it was something she'd believed was gone forever.

Adam was a wonderful lover. She'd forgotten what it was like to feel so possessed, so complete. But it wasn't just his physical prowess that had turned her world upside down. It was the man himself. He was strong yet gentle. Forthright yet shy. Headstrong yet sensitive. He was wounded, yet he was a healer.

And he was caring. What he had said about his father had moved her. She now understood why he was so protective toward Evelyn, although she was sure he would be the same attentive son under any circumstance.

Through the French doors she could see him lying in bed. A warm glow flowed through her. She was falling in love.

She hadn't meant for it to happen. Hadn't wanted it to happen. She could accept it or fight it, but she couldn't deny that it existed. Love wasn't something that could be ordered or canceled at will. And, she thought with regrets, if rooted in a secret, it wasn't something that would grow.

She leaned against the railing and once again looked up at the sky. "Star light, star bright, first star I see tonight…" But it was too late for wishes. The first star had already been in the sky for hours, and like the flame on a candle that was burning low, it would soon vanish.

If she *could* have a wish, what would she wish for?

She wanted Megan and she wanted Adam. There was only one wish that could give her both. She would wish that among all Adam's endearing traits, understanding was one of his strongest.

She resolved to tell him the whole story, as soon as he woke up.

He opened his eyes and reached for her. She wasn't there, and for a moment he was anxious. But then he looked up and saw her. The doors to the balcony were open, and in the dim light he could make out her silhouette, the thin fabric of her robe shimmering in the early dawn. Standing there, she was so beautiful he was afraid to breathe. He was worried that even the slightest change in the air would cause her to turn around, and he wasn't ready to relinquish this picture of her.

Soon he would have to go home. Act as if nothing had changed. Or did he? Why should he pretend?

He'd called Paula some time last night to tell her he wouldn't be back until morning. She hadn't asked any questions, but he'd sensed that she'd known what was happening.

So why did he feel the need to hide it?

Because it was insane. It was too soon. It was too early for him to be having the kind of thoughts he was having. This sort of thinking could lead to panty hose in his bathroom, cosmetics across his dresser, and he wasn't ready. He groaned. He couldn't believe he'd said "not right away" to her worry about getting pregnant.

Don't think with the wrong head, his father had said.

It was almost Saturday morning. He knew that his mother and Megan would sleep in late. If he arrived home before they awoke, they wouldn't know he'd been gone all night.

As though sensing his gaze, Rachel turned around. She walked back to him, removed her robe and crawled into bed beside him.

"Adam, we need to talk."

Suddenly he was afraid she was thinking the same thing he was. "Later," he murmured, and lowered his lips on hers.

He knew that if he lived to be a hundred, he would never grow tired of kissing her. Her lips were soft and inviting, as if they'd been molded especially for his. But the softness of her lips wasn't the reason he was kissing her now.

He didn't want her to speak. He wanted to hold on to the moment just a little longer.

He didn't say the words he'd been thinking, and neither did she.

Chapter Ten

She'd almost told him. She'd almost told him her secret, but reality had stopped her. Reality being his kiss, his touch, the time they'd spent in each other's arms. Nearly two weeks had passed since that first night, and reality was still interfering.

And what a reality it was, Rachel thought, feeling a wave of heat surge all the way to her toes. The nights that had followed that first one had been filled with lovemaking, Adam leaving her apartment shortly after daybreak. Not to mention the lunch hours they'd spent after sneaking out of the center, back to her bed. She hadn't done much skating these days, but she certainly wasn't suffering from a lack of exercise.

Exercise? She could be in training for the sexual Olympics! She felt her color rise as she entered the women's dressing room, still thinking about their vigorous schedule. She checked through the costumes, making sure nothing was missing. Darn. She had pinned Annie's name tag to the wrong costume. I have to concentrate, she reprimanded herself, or I'll have Miss Hannigan wearing Annie's red wig. But it was no use. Adam's face kept popping up in her mind.

It was going so well...he was so close...so close to saying those three magic words. Wouldn't it be better to wait until he'd said them before she spilled the beans? Those three little words would be an insurance policy. No matter how angry he'd be, he'd forgive her if he loved her.

She forced herself back to the task at hand. Can't have a redheaded Miss Hannigan, she thought. Can't have Grace Farrel's hair looking like a dirty dishrag, either. She placed a cardboard box on the closet's top shelf and smiled to herself, thinking of her purchase. She'd looked in all the thrift shops for a brunette wig but hadn't found anything suitable. The center had a small assortment of costume wigs, including a red hairpiece that she'd imaginatively fixed up for Annie, but the only dark wig was part of a witch's outfit. She'd tried to style it, but it still looked more like a horse's tail than hair. Finally she'd decided to buy a new one. She would surprise Megan with it—and with something else she had bought—at the dress rehearsal tomorrow.

All the other cast mothers had dug into their own pockets for their children's costumes. Why shouldn't she?

"Are you ready?" Megan asked, standing in the doorway.

"Perfect timing," Rachel said, stepping into the hallway. She locked the door behind her and dropped the keys into her skirt pocket. "I just need to get my purse, and we're off. I hope you're hungry. I want to try that

ELISSA AMBROSE 189

new Italian bistro. I hear the pasta is so good, you can put on five pounds just by reading the menu.'' Adam had pretended to be disappointed that Rachel had made other plans for lunch, but she knew he was pleased she was spending so much time with Megan. Besides, she'd promised to make it up to him later....

Megan was unusually quiet as they headed backstage. It's just nerves, Rachel thought. Everyone in the cast was a little edgy, now that they were so close to the opening night on Friday. For some it would be their first production, but even for the young actors who had performed before, there was no avoiding opening-night jitters.

Rachel approached her desk. And stopped. Something was wrong.

''Oh, no,'' Megan whispered behind her. ''Not you.''

The desk drawer gaped open, its lock broken. Rachel's purse was gone.

What a coup on his part, considering the tight budget—just look at the way they had to scrounge for costumes! Adam hung up the phone, feeling a sense of accomplishment. The council had just agreed to his recommendations, and in the fall two new programs would be implemented. First, the center would be hosting day care for seniors with Alzheimer's who still maintained a manageable level of functioning. Providing much needed socialization, the program would offer structured activities while at the same time encouraging independence. Adam's mood dropped. Unfortunately this program would be of no use to his mother. Evelyn's condition had worsened considerably over the past few weeks, her wanderings becoming excessive, the incontinence chronic. But thinking of the second program, he brightened. The center would be conducting a support group for those involved in the care-giving process. He believed that they would greatly benefit by sharing their experiences.

In addition to his busy schedule, Adam was actively involved in the production of *Annie*. The center was buzzing with excitement, the scenery built and painted, the props almost completed. People were coming and going all week, bringing in materials, shouting orders. When he wasn't at the center, or at home, he was with Rachel. Since their first night together, he couldn't get enough of her.

He knew he was going too fast. He'd never been one to rush into things, but these days he was acting like a racehorse wearing blinders. It's back to those blinders, he thought wryly. He'd tried to tell himself he had to slow down, but whenever he was with her, all his solid reasoning turned to sawdust.

He was getting tired of all the sneaking around, but what choice did he have? Until he knew where their relationship was headed, it would have to remain undisclosed. What if it ended? He knew that Megan and Rachel were growing closer; why get Megan's hopes up?

A knock on the office door jolted him out of his thoughts. "It's open!" he called.

Rachel stood in the doorway, hesitating. He rose to his feet and took her in his arms, kicking the door closed behind her. He pressed his mouth down on hers, abandoning all thoughts of sawdust and racehorses.

"We have a problem," she said, breathless, after he finally released her.

"We have a problem all right. The problem is that we're stuck in this building when we could be at your apartment, finishing what we've started." He lowered his head to kiss her again, but she pulled away and looked up at him.

Here it comes, he thought. Here comes the part where she tells me she's a felon on the run, or worse, she still has a husband stashed away in Hartford.

"My purse is missing."

He paused, not comprehending, and then realized she wasn't revealing some deep, dark secret. "What do you mean, 'missing'? Did you leave it somewhere?"

"Someone broke into my desk. My purse is gone."

"If it's not one thing, it's something else," he grumbled, reaching for the phone. "First the sound system goes on the fritz and then the air-conditioning breaks down. Now, it seems, the Middlewood Minor Mob has found its way to the center. It's time Megan stopped playing her little games. If she knows anything at all, she'd better speak up." He punched in Doreen's extension. "Doreen, can you get Megan in here?"

"I already spoke to Megan," Rachel said, placing her hand on his arm. "We need to talk."

"Never mind," he spoke into the phone, then put it down. He motioned for Rachel to sit and took the chair beside her. "Go on."

"Megan was with me when I went to get my purse. One of the first things she said was that I should change the lock on my front door at home, and it struck me as odd that she was so insistent. She assumed that whoever took my purse had my keys and address, but I assured her that I carry my key ring with me all the time." She let out a long sigh. "I know what's going on, Adam. When I questioned her further, she broke down and told me. I think she was afraid I would be the next target."

His face fell. "So she *is* involved."

"No, Adam, she's not, but she told me who is. It's

that older boy, Brandon Porter. She says that he's the one who took my bag. There've been so many strangers in the center today, he probably figured he could slip by unnoticed.''

''Mark Porter's son? The Porters are one of the wealthiest families in Middlewood. Why would he steal? That kid has everything money can buy.''

''I can think of many reasons why he would steal, but I suspect that money has nothing to do with it.''

Adam stared out the window, weighing her words. If money had nothing to do with it, then what did? A lack of communication at home? A lack of understanding? His thoughts returned to Megan. If he'd been more understanding, would he and Rachel be having this conversation now?

''It seems that Erika's wasn't the only place broken into with a key,'' Rachel continued. ''Two other households were robbed, and both use Sharon Pickart as their housecleaner. Megan thinks that the keys came from Sharon's daughter, Jane, although she insists that Jane had nothing to do with the actual robberies. Sharon cleans offices downtown three nights a week, and some of the kids meet at her house when she's out. Megan thinks that somehow Brandon got hold of the keys and made copies.''

''What I don't understand is why Megan wouldn't come to me. I don't know why she even hangs out with these kids.''

''They're not all bad,'' Rachel said. ''Most of them are just troubled. That's what drew them to each other in the first place. They call themselves the Misfits Club, isn't that awful? It's funny how kids can sense this kind of thing, this need to bond with others who feel the same way. They started out together for company, and then, to alleviate their boredom, or maybe blow off some steam, they started pulling minor pranks. Even when the pranks became serious, like egging cars, kids like Megan and Jane—basically good kids who desperately want to belong somewhere—didn't drop out of the club.''

''She belongs at home,'' Adam said tightly. ''With me. I give her everything she needs.'' He was sure that Rachel was thinking of his earlier decision to send Megan away to school. But all that was history. In any case, Megan's behavioral problems had started long before he'd even considered it.

''She needs to know you're not going to leave her. She needs to know you won't die. Unfortunately, you can't promise her that. No one can.''

''What else did she say?'' he asked, unnerved.

''When Brandon broke into the first apartment, most of the kids got scared and wanted out of the club. He never actually admitted to committing the robberies, but he made it clear that if they said anything, he would get back at them. He told Jane that if the burglar were caught, her mother would never be able to find work again. He told Megan that the burglar could get so angry, he might—and these are his exact words, according to Megan—feel the need to hurt Cinnamon. You've seen him. He's fourteen, and big for his age. He's been held back twice already in school. The others are terrified of him.''

''If Megan is so afraid, why is she speaking up now?''

''She saw him sneaking around in the hallway. He told her if anyone suspected him, she'd be blamed, too. And now that she knows the truth, he wants her help with the robberies. It seems that he and his buddies could use more hands.''

''And all this has been happening under our noses.

Where have I been all this time? How could I have been so blind? I'm glad she feels she can talk to you, at least. It's obvious she doesn't trust me.''

"Sometimes kids see parents as their worst enemies," Rachel said, smiling sadly. "It's part of growing up. She'll find her way back to you." She reached for his hand. "I know how difficult this is for you, but none of it is your fault. You've brought her up well, Adam. She's a brave young woman. In spite of Brandon's threats, she knew she couldn't steal."

"You're right about one thing. She's a good kid. But I should have figured out what was going on." Once again he picked up the phone. "We have to report this to the police."

"Ever since the center opened, it's been one crisis after another."

The song of the cicadas drifted in through the open French doors, the curtains rustling in the breeze. She snuggled closer to him in her bed, cradling against his chest. "It hasn't been that bad. You're just feeling stressed out, what with all the new projects you have on your plate. And because of *Annie.* But tomorrow is Thursday, full dress rehearsal. The air-conditioning and sound system are working fine again, and we're in the final stretch."

"And that's another thing," he said. "This play."

"All right, so there've been a few minor glitches, like Cinny chewing up Annie's sweater, and Daddy War-bucks coming down with a cold. But we're over all that, and we're almost there. It's going to be a great success, you'll see."

"That's not what I'm talking about. I'm talking about the story behind the play. I have to tell you, Rachel, I was never happy about the committee's choice to begin with.''

Her heart thumped inside her chest. So it was back to that. ''Are we talking about Pandora's box again?''

''I'm talking about the moral issues in the story. I'm not sure I like what the play teaches. It emphasizes taking the easy way out, and Megan is very impressionable. For instance, a couple of weeks ago she told me she was going to ask Erika to drop one of the dance routines. She was having difficulty learning the steps, and rather than working harder, she wanted to give up.''

Rachel shifted out of his arms. ''The first time we discussed these so-called issues, I believe you used the words *negative values.* And I still don't agree with you. I don't think this play is responsible for Megan's attitude. It's just a story, remember?''

''Yeah, I remember. Escapism. Entertainment. But what kind of parents would give away their child just because they were broke? What kind of moral is that? If everyone during the Depression gave up so easily, the orphanages would have been bursting with kids.''

''What do you know about it?'' she shot back without thinking. ''Do you have any idea what it was like not being able to care for your child, giving her away because you knew it was the only way she would have a chance in this world? Bursting orphanages! Don't you think you're being a little harsh?''

''Okay, so sometimes I'm judgmental. So sue me. It's just that I hate it when people give up.''

She held back her retort. She'd managed to set him on the right path—the road to matrimony—and antagonizing him was not the wisest way to keep him steered in that direction. But he'd brought the subject up, and time was running out. This was as good an opening as any to tell him who she was.

She held her breath, then released it slowly. "Sometimes people have no choice," she began, trying to ignore the tightening in her throat. "A while ago you said you were afraid that Megan would open Pandora's box. Afraid she might get it in her head to look for her natural mother. Tell me, Adam, what if she did? Would it really be so bad?"

He looked at her as if she'd lost her mind. "What kind of mother would abandon her baby? In my book, only an uncaring, self-serving person could commit such an act."

Rachel recalled what Megan had said to her on the night of the center's opening. *In my book, you don't give people away like used clothes.*

She sat up and reached for her robe at the foot of the bed. "I need some air."

"Now I've upset you." He tried to take her arm, but she shrugged him away, refusing to look at him. "Come on, Rachel, what's going on? I can't believe you're upset just because we happen to disagree about the play."

Stop it, she chastised herself. What did you expect? That you could just say it and everything would be rosy? No one said it was going to be easy.

And no one said she had to tell him this instant, either.

"Why did it have to be Connors and Reynolds who came to the center?" she asked, abruptly changing the subject. "You'd think they were the only officers on the force. I was never so embarrassed! They looked at me as though they expected me to light up like a Christmas tree."

"No, I think they were expecting you to quack up," he said with a straight face.

At least they were no longer talking about Megan's adoption, even if she'd had to make herself the brunt of a joke to achieve this. "You want a Christmas tree?" she asked, forcing herself to be playful. "I'll give you a Christmas tree." She pulled the bed linen over her head and stuck out her arms. He laughed and pulled her on top of him, tangling them both in the sheet. In spite of her mood, she found herself laughing along with him.

A thought occurred to her and she sobered. She sat up, removing the sheet from her head. "What's going to happen to Brandon? He won't have to go to jail, will he? Everyone deserves a second chance."

"I should have known you'd take the side of the underdog, but I'm not complaining. It's part of what makes you special." He planted a kiss on her nose. "There'll be a hearing in juvenile court, and he'll probably be put on probation. Of course, there's the matter of remuneration, and a little community service would do him a world of good. Since this is his first offense, I doubt he'll be sent to a detention facility."

"How do you know it's his first offence?"

"After you left my office, your friend Connors told me that they'd already questioned Sharon, since she had keys to the three apartments that were robbed without forced entry. They'd also looked into the records of everyone associated with her, including her daughter and the kids she hangs out with."

Another thought entered her mind, this one more disturbing. "What about Megan? Isn't she some kind of accessory?"

"Considering the way Brandon threatened her, I doubt the judge will see it that way. But she still has to deal with me."

Rachel folded her arms across her chest. "You go

easy on her, Adam, do you hear? The reason she didn't speak up earlier was because she was afraid. And she didn't even know it was Brandon, not for sure, until today.''

"Maybe so, but I'm going to watch over her carefully. I want to know where she is, every minute."

"What, and treat her like a prisoner? Why don't you just put her under house arrest?" She aimed her finger at him. "You've got to trust her, Adam. Remember, she did come forward, and that took courage."

"Okay, I get your point," he said, biting her finger playfully. "But I still want to know everything she does, everyone she talks to. Like I said, she's very impressionable."

"Why don't you pitch a tent outside her window? I'll bring you coffee and a clean pair of underwear every morning. Would that make you happy?"

He gave her his boyish smile. "Hey, did I ever tell you I used to be a Boy Scout? I know all about pitching tents."

She rolled her eyes. "Yeah, I remember. Boy Scout as in helping elderly women cross the street. The kind of Pollyanna image you're trying to promote."

"Forget Pollyanna," he said, throwing the sheet across his lap. "How do you like my tent?"

Something was bothering Rachel.

Adam awoke with this on his mind, just as the sun was rising. Rays of light peeked in through the curtains, promising warm sunshine and clear blue skies. It hadn't rained in days, and today would be no exception.

Then again, he knew how deceptive blue skies could be.

He looked over at her sleeping beside him, wondering

if she was dreaming. It disturbed him that she wouldn't confide in him. He reached across to touch her forehead, as though he could magically wipe away her worries.

He couldn't stand knowing that she was suffering.

He wanted to hold her, to tell her that he would take care of her, that he would always be there for her. For better or worse, he thought, then tried to dismiss the notion.

Slow down, he reminded himself.

He knew that Rachel had been expecting him to say those three magic words. Expecting some kind of commitment. He saw it in her eyes. He saw it every time he took her in his arms. But with each passing moment, Cathy was slipping farther away, and he was afraid of losing her forever. She'd been the love of his life. The girl he'd teased all through grade school, at twelve his best friend, later his teenage sweetheart. How could he let her go as if she'd never existed?

He wanted to keep things with Rachel just the way they were.

Was that what was bothering her? Maybe, but there was something else, as well. Something she was keeping inside. She was hiding something, had been from the start. He figured she would tell him sooner or later, but part of him hoped she never would. It was as though he sensed the truth would cause his world to cave in.

He resisted the urge to scoop her up in his arms, knowing where that would lead. He wanted to get back home before Megan woke up. Which was crazy. Paula knew where he went each night, and it wouldn't be long before Megan caught on, too. But as long as he didn't bring it out into the open, he could pretend it wasn't real. As long as it remained only fantasy, it could endure.

Maybe he didn't want to know what was bothering

her. Maybe he didn't want to deal with the truth just yet. Maybe he knew that the truth would change everything.

She turned over in bed, murmuring something he couldn't make out. He leaned over again and brushed her lips with his, and then as quietly as possible, crept out of bed and prepared to leave.

Rachel was sitting at her desk when Erika approached her.

"Looking for this?"

"My purse!" Rachel said. "Where did you find it?" She made a motion to take it, but Erika stepped back, clutching the leather bag.

"You should be more careful where you leave your things," Erika said, opening the clasp. "They could fall into the wrong hands. I found this on top of the vending machine, after you had gone home yesterday. If you had stayed to help out with the props, you might have found it yourself. But no, you and your soon-to-be-ex-boyfriend—"

"Give me my purse."

"Oh, I will, don't worry. After you've heard what I have to say. You are interested, aren't you?" When Rachel didn't answer, Erika smiled and continued. "Of course you are. When I saw the purse on top of the machine, I knew it looked familiar, but I had to make sure it was yours. So I opened it. But there was no wallet, which didn't surprise me. It's the first thing a thief would take."

Rachel glared at her. "Get to the point. Some of us have work to do."

"Maybe you should remember that the next time you sneak out of here and leave me alone to run this place. And don't think people don't know what's going on.

Don't think they're not talking about how you've sleazed up to the boss.''

"What I do on my time is no one's business but mine," Rachel retorted. She stood up and made another swipe at the purse, but Erika raised it over her head, out of Rachel's reach.

"Now where was I?" Erika said, smirking. "Right. No wallet. Then I saw this picture of you—" she pulled out a photograph from the purse "—and Megan standing in front of a fireplace. A lit fireplace. I thought it was odd, considering it's summer. I turned the picture around and wouldn't you know it, there was something written on the back." She handed the photograph to Rachel. "Read it."

Rachel didn't have to read it to know what it said. The words were inscribed on her memory as clearly as the writing on the picture. Even though sentimentality wasn't something her mother had normally succumbed to, she must have been in a sentimental mood when she'd written them. Maybe she'd just finished rehearsing a Chopin nocturne or a lullaby by Brahms, but whatever the reason for the break in character, Rachel didn't care. The words had sustained her through many hard years, and she carried the picture with her everywhere.

"You don't want to read it? Doesn't matter. I have a good memory. It says, 'Beth and Rachel Cunningham, mother and daughter, me and my darling princess.' Talk about hokey. I can practically hear violins." The mockery in her eyes gave way to a cold gleam. "It appears that Evelyn isn't so crazy, after all. Beth Cunningham, she called you, that day she decided to soak the stage. You're not the woman in this picture, Beth is. Your mother. You're the child, not Megan. I know everything, Rachel. After I found your purse, I made a few calls. It wasn't hard to put two and two together. I know about your pregnancy and I know about Megan.''

"I suppose you're going to tell Adam," Rachel said, fighting panic.

She laughed. "You *are* naive. Why should I be the bad guy? Adam will know soon enough. This isn't something you can hide forever—look how easily I found out. And when he does learn the truth, guess who's going to be around to pick up the pieces? But trust me, if he doesn't discover the truth on his own, I'm going to make damn sure he finds out." She slammed the purse into Rachel's hands. "Here, take it. It's no wonder the thief didn't keep it. A piece of trash like this can be found at any thrift shop for under a dollar."

Rachel was shaking so hard, she couldn't believe her own voice when she said, "You would know all about that. When it comes to trash, you're the expert."

She was still steaming as she headed toward the women's dressing room. Erika was a real piece of work. It was a good thing Adam had finally seen through her, Rachel thought. She could just imagine what their weekends might have been like, after she and Adam were married, with good old Aunt Ricky coming over for a barbecue, trying to sabotage Rachel at every turn.

Scheming, calculating, cunning.

Wait a minute. Just who was Rachel describing? She thought about the way she had plotted right from the start to be with her daughter, and realization sliced through her.

Was it really so wrong? Was it wrong to reach out for your child? Was it wrong to want something so badly, you almost believed you could hope it into being?

These were the questions she had asked herself after moving to Middlewood. Questions that until now had remained unanswered. If manipulation and deceit were wrong, then the answer to these questions was an unqualified yes.

She was no better than Erika.

This time when the guilt assailed her, she didn't will it away. Didn't want to will it away. She had let her obsession with her daughter blind her to everything else, including common decency, but she couldn't ignore the guilt any longer.

She entered the dressing room, and with a heavy heart began to set up for the dress rehearsal. As she laid the makeup out in trays, she thought about her marriage. She had never told her husband about the baby she had given up. He had found out after mistakenly opening the letter from the agency—the letter addressed to her stating that no information regarding her daughter could be released.

Her husband had been furious. Not because of Rachel's past, but because she had never told him. A marriage without trust is no marriage at all, he'd said.

Trust. She'd accused him of spying on her, and he'd accused her of lying. The argument that had followed had been the beginning of the end.

Trust. Adam didn't deserve to be lied to. No one did. How could a relationship that was built on lies survive?

She knew he was in the men's dressing room, preparing for the dress rehearsal just as she was doing in here. All she had to do was unlock the adjoining door and go in there. The cast wouldn't be arriving for another half hour. She and Adam would have time to talk.

Thirty minutes weighed against a lifetime.

She opened the door and stepped into the room. Two heads turned. Erika and Adam looked at her blandly.

"Uh, excuse me," Rachel stammered. "You're busy. I'll come back later."

She felt a churning in her stomach. Seconds later she was in the ladies' lounge, choking back nausea. Erika hadn't meant it when she said she wouldn't tell him. And now, because the truth hadn't come from Rachel, Adam would doubt that she had ever intended to tell him. He would never trust her again.

Thirty minutes later she still hadn't budged from the couch in the lounge, fear twisting around her heart, preventing her from moving. No, not fear. Sheer terror. Not only could she lose her daughter, she could lose the man she loved.

Adam knew.

She glanced at the clock. It was show time. She splashed cold water on her face and headed back to the women's dressing room. Adam was coming from the auditorium, his shoulders hunched with stress.

"Erika told me about the sound system," he groaned when he saw her. "That annoying hum is back. Tell me something, why are full dress rehearsals always such catastrophes?"

Relief flooded through her. Erika hadn't told him. But another emotion filled her, taking her by surprise. "Is that what you and Erika were discussing? The sound system?" She immediately regretted her tone. Why shouldn't Adam talk to Erika? They worked together. In fact, Rachel admired his ability to keep his personal problems and business life separate. As for her, talking to Erika was like having a root canal.

He laughed heartily. "Do I detect a note of jealousy? I think I like it. It means you care. And you look good in green. Goes with your eyes."

"Of course I care. And for your information, I am not jealous."

He kissed her on the nose, amusement shining in his

eyes. He was developing a penchant for this particular mode of expression, and she wasn't sure she liked it. But at the moment she was too grateful to complain. She'd been given a reprieve. She would tell him everything tonight at her apartment, when the strain of the rehearsal was behind him. When Erika was the furthest thing from his mind.

"Where were you?" Megan asked nervously when Rachel had returned to the dressing room. "Everyone's already in costume, and we haven't even started my makeup. If we rush it, I'm going to end up looking like an old hag."

"We have plenty of time," Rachel reassured her. "And I promise, you're going to look beautiful." Keep smiling, she reminded herself. Keep smiling, even though everything you treasure might soon be taken away.

"Erika said she'd do my makeup, but I told her to forget it. She's doing Alice's."

Across the room, Erika lifted her head and waved at Rachel.

Ignoring her, Rachel opened the closet door and pulled down the box she had put away the day before. She motioned for Megan to sit at the dressing table. "Before we start with the makeup, I have a surprise for you." She lifted the wig out of the box.

"It's stunning! So dark and silky, and so grown-up! I was afraid I'd have to wear that ugly old mop. This is perfect."

"There's something else in the box, too," Rachel said, pulling out a small paper bag. "I know how much you wanted to wear something fancier with your costume. Something that would make you look older." She handed Megan the costume jewelry she had bought at

the thrift shop. "It wasn't expensive, and it's a little loud
with all those rhinestones. But this is the theater. We're
supposed to be loud. If you don't want to take off the
locket you've got on, you can tuck it in under your col-
lar."

"No, I can take it off. Will you keep it safe for me?"

After unclasping the locket and placing it in her
pocket, Rachel fastened the rhinestone necklace around
Megan's neck. "There. What do you think?"

"It's gorgeous!" Megan gushed. "Thank you, Rachel. You always know just the right thing to do. You
know what? Someday you're going to be a great mom."

All her life Rachel had wanted a daughter, but nothing
could have ever prepared her for the way she felt now,
hearing those words. "Let's get to work," she said, her
voice breaking. "First I'll do your makeup and then
we'll arrange the wig."

After the foundation came the eyeliner, then the
shadow. After that, mascara and blush. "You look so
much older," she said, becoming increasingly uneasy as
Megan's face matured under her touch. It was like
watching a Polaroid develop before her eyes.

The more it came into focus, the more unsettled Rachel felt.

Megan stared straight ahead at the mirror, not speaking. After Rachel had finished applying the lipstick, she
stood back and looked at her daughter's reflection.

So much older.

Their eyes met.

"Put the wig on," Megan said slowly. "Make sure
you cover all the red."

Rachel stood behind her daughter, paralyzed.

"Is everyone dressed in there?" Adam called through
the adjoining door. "Can I come in?"

"Come on in, Adam," Erika sang back. "Everyone's dressed. We're just about done."

Adam crossed the room and looked at Megan. "Wow!" he said appreciatively. "You look gorgeous! You look like—" He stopped, his eyes widening.

"Put the wig on," Megan repeated.

With shaky hands, Rachel picked up the wig and placed it on Megan's head.

Four faces stared out at Rachel from the mirror. Erika was wearing that sickly sweet smile, and Adam had turned a pasty white. Megan's eyes never left Rachel's.

Two of the reflections were identical.

Chapter Eleven

This couldn't be happening.

It was as if he were watching a movie in slow motion. Maybe, he thought with cold detachment, this was nature's way of allowing him to assess the situation, as in an accident when an eternity goes by before the oncoming vehicle crashes into the side of your car. You can practically see the eyes of the other driver, as if his body is right there with you in the front seat, and it dawns on you that you have time. Time to consider your options: should I veer to the left or to the right? Should I slam on the brakes?

Rachel was Megan's mother. It was as clear to him as her eyes in the mirror—direct, green eyes that, as much as he had tried to fight it, had caught him under their spell. The same eyes she had bequeathed to Megan.

Why hadn't he noticed the similarity before? He felt like a fool. She'd been using him to get to his daughter.

She was no better than Erika. Both women had been using him to get what they wanted.

A sickening realization washed over him. Megan wasn't Rachel's prime objective. Like Erika, she was after his money.

The wheels under Megan's chair squealed as she pushed away from the dressing table, the sound speeding up time once again. "Now I know why you've been acting so nice to me," she said to Rachel in a low, controlled voice. "It all makes sense. You want to be my mother. Well, I have news for you. I already had a mother. You made your choice a long time ago when you threw me away."

"Megan, please—"

Megan shoved away Rachel's hand, all pretense of calm abandoned. "Don't touch me! Stay away from me! You're not my mother—my mother would never have given me away!" She pulled the wig from her head and threw it onto the dressing table. "And you can take back this stupid wig. How can I wear it now? Everyone would *know.* Dad, make her go away, before they all find out! She's not my mother—my mother is dead!" She tore off her smock and ran across the room, Rachel scrambling after her.

With two long strides Adam was at the door, restraining Rachel with a hand on her arm. "Didn't you hear her? She wants you to stay away."

"Let me go to her, Adam. I need to talk to her. I need to make her understand."

"It's a little late for talking, or for anything else you might have in mind. You didn't want her when she was born, and now suddenly you've had a change of heart? What made you think you could just come walking into her life? Sorry, Rachel. Like Megan said, it doesn't work that way.''

''This isn't just some whim! I've *always* wanted her. I *had* to give her up.''

He was sure that everyone was listening. Erika was standing behind Alice Tucker, fiddling with the curly red wig. He looked in the mirror where Alice was sitting, and what he saw startled him. On Erika's lips was an ugly, twisted smile.

''Who else knows?'' he hissed.

''No one, Adam. I promise. No one except Erika. And Doreen.''

''Is there anyone who *doesn't* know?'' He stuck his head out into the corridor to make sure Megan was gone. ''Come with me,'' he ordered Rachel, seizing her by the elbow and steering her toward the cafeteria.

The large room was abandoned. He led her to the back and faced her. He wanted to shake her until her teeth rattled, but he wasn't a violent man. He gripped her shoulders, then dropped his hands as if the skin under her blouse had burned his fingers. He couldn't bear to touch her, now or ever again. ''Did you really think you could get away with it? Did you think I wouldn't find out?''

''I was going to tell you,'' she answered in a tremulous voice, her face as pale as his had been a moment ago in the mirror. ''I just needed time to make you…to make you trust me.''

He might have laughed if he hadn't been so angry. ''*Trust* you? Did you really think that after I found out I could *trust* you?''

''I was wrong, but I didn't know what else to do. Two years ago you made it clear that you would never let me into Megan's life. I was desperate. I couldn't think of any other way to convince you."

"Don't give me that," he snarled. "It's obvious what's going on. You thought that because you're Megan's mother, you had a ticket to Easy Street. It's bad enough that you tried to use me, but to use your own daughter! What kind of woman are you?"

"No, Adam! You've got it all wrong! All I wanted was to be with Megan. I knew she was having problems and I wanted to be with her. I wanted to help her, but I had no idea where she even lived. And I didn't know about the money." Suddenly her eyes lit up. "I can prove it to you," she said excitedly. "I have all the reports and receipts from the private investigator. Why would I hire a P.I. if I had known who you were? All I wanted was to find my daughter, and I had no idea what I would learn when I hired him. He didn't even mention the inheritance. I learned about that from Doreen."

"You hired a private investigator? You had me *followed?*"

"No! I hired him to find Megan. I thought I had no choice."

"There are always choices. Always options. And your story is full of holes. For instance, before you hired the P.I., how did you know that Megan was having problems?"

Her gaze dropped. "I had a...feeling."

"You had a feeling," he scoffed. "I suppose this is where you tell me it was a mother's intuition. The same intuition that led you to give her up in the first place."

"It wasn't intuition twelve years ago and it was more than intuition that made me go looking for her. Twelve years ago I did what I did because I had no choice.

Contrary to what you believe, sometimes a person *has* no other choice. I did it for Megan.''

He remembered a previous conversation they'd had regarding the adoption issue in *Annie*. She'd been so defensive, so adamant. She'd truly believed that what Annie's mother had done, she'd done for the sake of her child. ''Okay, I'll play along. If it wasn't intuition that made you go out and hire a P.I., then what was it?''

She hesitated. ''You won't believe me.''

Her eyes met his, and for a moment he thought he could believe anything she might tell him. ''Try me,'' he said, wanting to trust in her again.

''It was the dreams. I started having dreams about her, dreams that warned me that she needed help. I learned later that the dreams were true.''

''Dreams,'' he repeated. ''You've been having dreams.'' He was immediately brought back to his senses, contempt replacing hope. ''I have to admit, for a moment you almost had me. For a moment I thought you might be telling the truth. Considering your track record, I realize the notion is preposterous.'' He took a step back. ''I want you out of here. Now. Megan wants nothing to do with you, and neither do I.''

''Are you *firing* me?''

It was almost déjà vu. He'd had a similar scene with Erika after the argument in her apartment. He knew he had no legal basis for firing Rachel, just as he'd had no legal basis for firing Erika. ''No, you're quitting,'' he replied, his body tense with outrage. ''If you care about my daughter one-tenth as much as you're trying to make me believe, you'll leave of your own accord. I don't want you causing her any more pain.''

''Megan's had a shock, but she'll come around. I just have to make her understand why I gave her up. Please,

Adam, give me a chance. I've always loved her, even before she was born. Giving her up was the hardest thing I ever did—but it doesn't mean I stopped caring.''

''My daughter doesn't need the kind of love you're offering. In my book lying and love don't mix. How do you expect her to trust you? How do you expect *me* to trust you?''

Before she could reply, he turned on his heel and left. As far as he was concerned, there was no answer.

The dress rehearsal was a disaster. The cast kept forgetting their lines, and the sound system hadn't been repaired yet. But for Rachel, that wasn't the worst of it. Wearing the converted witch's wig, Megan had acted her role as though her heart wasn't in it. When Annie sang ''Maybe,'' Megan burst into tears backstage. Cinnamon trotted over to lick her hands, but Megan angrily pushed her away. Barking excitedly, the puppy jumped into the audience and raced to Evelyn, who was sitting with Paula in the auditorium.

''I told Adam not to let his mother watch,'' Erika grumbled, ''but did he listen? Does he ever listen?''

Rachel ignored her. Adam had been worried that his mother would cause a disturbance during the actual performance, and so when Paula arrived with Evelyn to drop off Cinnamon, he had asked her to stay. That way, Evelyn could watch the rehearsal. ''I want my mother to see Megan onstage,'' he'd told Rachel earlier that morning. ''She might not be the woman she once was, but she'll always be Megan's grandmother.''

Had it only been this morning when he'd said those words? Had it only been this morning when he'd last kissed her? And she didn't mean on her nose. It was as if an eon had passed since then, as if in the interim an ice age had wiped out her entire world, all her hopes and dreams.

After rehearsal, Rachel headed straight for Adam's office. Take a deep breath, she instructed herself. He didn't mean the things he said. Now that he was over the initial shock, they'd have a long talk. He would see her side of it. She'd make sure of it.

"He's already gone," Doreen said, as Rachel passed her desk. "He and Megan left a few minutes ago. Why don't you try him on his cell?"

"He'll hang up," Rachel said miserably. "Right now I'm the last person he wants to talk to. I was hoping to catch him before he left. It's easier to make someone listen in person." Suddenly the stress of the day caught up with her and she felt the onset of tears.

But the tears wouldn't come. Instead she let out a wrenching sob, and Doreen immediately stood up to hug her. "I knew this would happen. I tried to warn you. I wanted you to tell him right from the start." She released Rachel and said matter-of-factly, "What's done is done. Now we have to figure out a way to make it better."

"You know what happened," Rachel said quietly.

"The whole center knows. The gossipmongers are having a field day. As far as they're concerned, this situation has been far more entertaining than *Annie*."

"He wants me to go away. He doesn't want me in Megan's life." Or his, Rachel thought with a fresh wave of despair.

"He's questioning the kind of mother you'd make."

"Because I gave up Megan."

"Because you lied. To Megan, to him, to everyone."

"Maybe he's right. Maybe I should leave. You once told me that no one can make him do anything he doesn't want to do, and that includes seeing my side of it.'' She remembered Adam's words and added, ''I don't want to cause Megan any more pain.''

Doreen placed her hands on Rachel's shoulders, staring her squarely in the eye. ''You want to run away? You think that's the answer? Right now your daughter is angry and confused, but she needs you. You wouldn't be here if you thought otherwise. If you go, you'll leave her in an even worse place than before. You can turn this thing over and over in your mind until you go crazy, asking yourself if you did the right thing by coming here, but the fact is, you did come here and you can't turn back the clock. You can't just pop into her life, turn her world upside down and then abandon her.''

''But Adam won't let me talk to her! And even if he does change his mind, she won't.'' She choked back another dry sob. ''She doesn't want me near her, and Adam told me to leave. He…he despises me.''

''He doesn't despise you. He's hurt. Don't run away, Rachel. Megan's not the only one who needs you.''

Rachel blinked with astonishment. ''I thought you were against me—you accused me of going after his money!''

''I was wrong. I just wanted to protect Adam, the same way he wants to protect Megan. He's been hit with a sledgehammer, but he's tough. He'll bounce back. Once he realizes he loves you—and right now, it seems he's the only person in Middlewood who doesn't realize it—he'll come around. If you leave, not only will you be abandoning your daughter, you'll be abandoning him. Won't you reconsider staying?''

Maybe I *should* stay, Rachel thought, at least until the play is over. She would have two more days to make Megan realize that she'd never meant to hurt her. Two more days to make Adam understand. If she failed, she would go back to Hartford. Go back and give them time to mull things over. A plan started jelling in her head. Gradually, she would start making contact. She could call Megan on her birthday in October, then she could speak to Adam about arranging a meeting, then she could—

No. No more plotting. She'd made her identity known, or rather, it had been made known for her, and there was nothing she could do or say to sway them. Adam and Megan had to come to terms with the truth on their own, and in their own time. And they would, she assured herself. They had to.

The ache inside her was saying something different. It was telling her that it wasn't going to happen. Telling her that she had lost her daughter and Adam forever.

"I can't stay," she answered, remembering how she had resolved, back in June, to leave Middlewood if her plan were to fail. *She couldn't spend the rest of her life looking around every corner, down every street, hoping to catch a glimpse of her daughter, living solely for those moments.*

Doreen gave her a half smile. "I'm afraid you have no choice. You made a commitment when you took on this job, and you have a responsibility to these kids. You have to stay, at least until the play is over."

"They don't need me here," Rachel protested. "They'll do just fine without me. My job as a coach is done."

"I don't think so. You saw how they kept forgetting their lines. Granted, it was probably due to dress-rehearsal jitters—that's why we have dress rehearsals, to iron out the wrinkles—but what if they forget their lines tomorrow? Who's going to stand backstage and prompt?

Who's going to bolster their confidence when they get nervous? Erika? I don't think so. They need you, Rachel, and you can't bail out now.''

The sound system was working again, the irritating static gone. None of the young actors forgot their lines, and Cinnamon was on her best behavior. In fact, the puppy all but stole the show, to Alice Tucker's vexation.

The play was a success. All three performances, opening night on Friday and the matinee and evening show on Saturday, had been completely sold out, which Rachel knew would mean a larger budget for the next production. Auditions for *Oliver* would be starting next week, and everyone at the center was already brimming with anticipation.

Everyone except her. She would be back in Hartford, teaching at the private school long before *Oliver* was staged. Although she'd told Adam she would be leaving when *Annie* was over, she'd been hoping that by then he would have relented. To add to her injury, she'd overheard Megan tell Doreen how glad she was that Rachel was going.

Alone backstage after Saturday night's performance, she could finally let down her guard. She could strip off the mask she'd been forced to wear these past two days. But still the tears wouldn't fall. She felt as numb as a wooden puppet.

From the top of her desk she picked up a bouquet of roses, which the cast had given her after the final curtain. She held it to her nose, but the flowers had no fragrance. She wasn't surprised. The numbness had taken hold of her entire body.

The sorrow was lodged deep inside, and inside she was crying.

A discarded script was lying on the floor backstage among an assortment of post-play debris—a pink bow, a single red slipper, a crumpled program. She put down the flowers and picked up the program. Megan had been wonderful, she thought, smoothing out the paper and tracing her finger across her daughter's name. A true actress, Megan had refused to let her distress interfere with her performance onstage. She'd even decided to wear the new wig, determined to give the role of Grace everything it deserved.

The show must go on, Rachel thought.

Too bad that her own acting skills were so limited. She was sure everyone could see through her frozen smile. She was sure everyone could see inside her, where her anguish lay raw and exposed.

She thought about those dreams people have, dreams in which they see themselves standing naked in a public place.

Exposed. Ashamed.

Yet in spite of her anguish, part of her was relieved. She was tired of secrets. The truth was out in the open, and whether or not Adam and Megan acknowledged it, there it was. She was Megan's mother.

Gathering her composure, she set off for the dressing room. One last task and she'd be out of their lives forever.

"Me, Rachel!" Alice implored. "Will you help me first?"

Rachel hesitated before approaching Alice's chair. I can't show any favoritism, she reminded herself. Not that Megan would let me near her.

"Close your eyes while I clean off the mascara," she told Alice, after dabbing a cotton ball with cold cream. "You were the best Annie I've ever seen," she added, and meant it. Like Megan, Alice was a natural-born actress, bent on making the stage her future.

"Are you coming to the cast party?" the ten-year-old asked expectantly.

Rachel was in no mood for festivity, but more significantly, she didn't want her presence to ruin the party for Megan. "I don't think so. I'd like to, but unfortunately something's come up."

"You have to come! We have a surprise for you! Everyone chipped in and Megan picked it out and—"

"Alice!" chimed in Margot Spelling, the girl who had played Miss Hannigan. "You weren't supposed to say anything! It's not a surprise if you tell!"

From her dressing table across the room, Megan looked over at Rachel. With her gaze on her daughter, Rachel said to Alice, "You already did so much. All of you did. Your performance was the best gift any drama coach could ever receive. And the flowers are beautiful."

Another bouquet of flowers, pink roses with baby's breath and ferns, lay across the dressing table where Doreen was removing Megan's makeup. *Megan didn't even look at me when I gave them to her,* Rachel thought, a fresh pain stabbing through her.

But she was looking at her now. Looking at her as if she wanted Rachel to speak.

It was all the invitation Rachel needed. She walked over to her daughter.

"You can go to the party if you want," Megan said, as though instinctively knowing why Rachel had declined. "I'm not going. My dad's going to drive me home."

"Don't be silly," Rachel said, her heart beating as

though it would break through her ribcage. "Everyone's expecting you, and you'll have a wonderful time."

Megan jutted out her half-cleaned chin. "No. I don't want to."

"Megan, please. I want you—"

"Leave me alone! I'm not going to the dumb party, and no one can make me!" With only half her face cleaned, still wearing her makeup smock, she got up to leave.

Tears threatened behind Rachel's eyelids, but still they refused to spill. She felt like a bow that had been stretched past its limit. She had to get out of there, had to get away before she completely snapped. She turned back to Alice. "I'm sorry, sweetheart. Someone else will have to finish up." At the door, something made her turn around. It wasn't anything she saw or heard; it was just a feeling. A feeling that caused her gaze to gravitate back toward Megan's table.

Megan had taken the flowers.

Renewed hope flooded through Rachel as she hurried along the corridor, looking for her daughter. And then she stopped. Adam was at the entrance, holding the door open for Megan.

"Adam, wait!"

"Let's go," Megan said, pulling on his sleeve as though she was three years old.

"Go to the car."

"But Dad—"

"*Now.*" His face softened. "I'll only be a minute. I promise."

Rachel waited for Megan to disappear into the parking lot. "Please, Adam, can't we at least talk about it?" She hated the pleading in her voice, hated the desperation, but she had to make him listen.

"There's nothing to talk about," he said in a dull voice. "You never gave a damn about Megan, and you sure as hell didn't give a damn about me."

"That's not true! I did...I do. I've always cared about Megan—she was all I could think about. I admit I didn't have feelings for you in the beginning, but then—" her voice dropped to a whisper "—something happened. I fell in love. I never thought I'd ever say those words again, but I'm in love with you, and the way I feel is not going to go away."

"How inconvenient for you," he said dryly. "But don't worry, I'm sure you'll make a speedy recovery. Too bad I can't say the same for Megan. Do you realize the harm you've caused? You've set her back months. All the progress she made has gone down the drain, because of your selfishness."

"It's just a minor setback," Rachel protested. "You know what they say, three steps forward, two steps back. She'll be all right, I promise. I wouldn't say it if I didn't believe it."

"You're one to make promises." He flashed her a look of disdain. "You want to know something funny? I wouldn't have stopped her if she'd wanted to see you. Whether I like it or not, and believe me I don't, you're her natural mother, and you're here. But she wants nothing to do with you, and I certainly won't force her to see you. Go back to Hartford, Rachel. There's nothing for you here."

He turned and walked out, taking her heart with him.

Her face was stinging with the tears that, until now, she'd been unable to release. Losing Adam and Megan was all she'd thought about since the truth had come out, and if she continued to dwell on it one minute longer, she would lose her mind. I have to do something, she told herself. I have to keep busy.

She had to clean out her locker and then her desk. Wiping away her tears, she walked through the passageway to the arena. She'd been leaving her purse in her locker since the theft of her wallet. She pulled it out, then picked up her skates, thinking of the first time she'd seen Adam out on the ice. She remembered how the sight of him had taken her breath away. Remembered how she'd felt wearing his sweatshirt, as if everything he was, everything he stood for, had been transferred from his soul to hers, like an unspoken promise.

Skates in one hand, purse in the other, she left the arena.

I have to keep busy, she reminded herself. I have to stop thinking about it. She knew what she'd be doing that night, to keep herself from brooding. She would be packing.

The dream had her in its grip, refusing to let her go. The voice in the night was so close, so loud, nothing like the song on the wind of two years ago, when the dreams first started.

Megan is in trouble.

She sat up with a start, still half-asleep. No more dreams, she told herself, as though she could will her subconscious into obedience. Go away, she ordered the now silent voice. Megan doesn't want me.

The doorbell jarred her into full wakefulness. She glanced at the clock on the bureau. Good Lord, it was after one! Who would ring her bell at this hour? With trepidation, she pulled on her robe, then tiptoed to the door.

"Dammit, Rachel. Open the door. It's Adam."

He stood on the landing, casually handsome in pleated khakis and an open suede jacket. He'd changed his clothes since the performance, she noted. His attire had definitely relaxed in the past few weeks. She wished he would apply his new, easy style to his belligerent attitude.

He glowered at her. "Are you going to ask me in, or do I have to stand here all night?"

"Oh, Adam, I'm so glad—"

"Save it," he said, brushing past her. "Doreen mentioned that you're leaving in the morning. I came by to bring you this." He handed her a gift-wrapped package. "It's a present from the cast. They were going to give it to you tonight at the party."

"I thought you had gone home," she said, remembering their scene at the entrance after the performance.

"After I took Megan home, I went back to the center. Unlike Megan, I didn't have the option of not going to the party. I stayed after everyone else had left, making sure all the props were stored away."

"You could have asked me for help," she reprimanded him lightly. "I would have been more than happy."

"I didn't need your help."

She stared down at the package in her hands, then looked up at him quizzically. "You came here in the middle of the night to bring me this?"

He looked flustered. "Look, it wasn't my idea. Megan made me promise that if you weren't at the party, I would make sure you got the present. She didn't want you to leave Middlewood without it."

"Megan made you promise?" she asked, hope stirring inside her. "Why would she do that? Are you saying she's having second thoughts?"

He glanced at the suitcases piled in the corner. "So it's true," he said, evading her questions. "You *are* leaving."

"Isn't that what you want?" She didn't even try to stop her next words. "Do you want me to stay? Just say the word. I can be unpacked in a minute."

"No. I want you to go, but unfortunately I'm not sure that's what my daughter wants. She still refuses to have anything to do with you, but I know her as if she were my own flesh and blood, and there's something she's not saying."

"Of course you know her," Rachel said softly. "You're her father."

"Look, this gift isn't the only reason I'm here. Right now Megan is hurt, but it's obvious she feels a bond with you. I know she's going to want to reestablish ties, and I came here to tell you I won't stand in your way. We can set up a meeting on her birthday, maybe even an occasional weekend. You're her mother, and I won't let my personal feelings interfere."

What he was offering was a hundred percent more than what she had a moment ago, and she was grateful, but she had been so sure that he'd come here to offer her more. She'd been so sure he'd come here to offer his heart. "You've told me what I want, and what you think Megan wants. What about you?"

"What I want is to forget you. To forget you ever came into my life."

Without warning, her anger rose to echo his. "I'm getting a little tired of your judgmental, self-righteous attitude. I admitted I was wrong. I *know* I was wrong. Not a minute goes by that I don't feel remorse for what I did, but if you were to ask me if I would do it over again, I'd have to say that I honestly don't know. All I could think about was that I had to be with my daughter. I had to help her. Yes, it was wrong, but what I did, I did out of love, not out of malevolence. Yet you're acting as if I'm some kind of monster.''

''Are you done?'' he asked flatly.

''No, I am *not* done. I have something else to say to you.'' She put the gift onto the counter and turned to him with determination. She'd told herself she wasn't going to do this. Wasn't going to try to sway him—she knew he had to work through his anger on his own before he could discard it—but she couldn't let him walk away, out of her life forever, without his knowing what was in her heart.

''I know that you and Cathy had a wonderful marriage,'' she began, ''and I'm grateful she was Megan's mother. I know she was a warm, nurturing person, and she'll always be the mother Megan remembers. She was the one who held Megan as a baby and rocked her to sleep at night. She was the one who took her to her first day of school. She's the reason Megan is who she is, the woman she's becoming. Cathy opened the way to her future, giving her the two most important tools in life—a strong mind and a good heart. I never wanted to replace her—and I was never after your money. I just wanted to be there for Megan, to guide her along her journey.''

''So you schemed your way into our lives.''

She winced. ''I devised a plan. I told myself that if you and Megan didn't accept me by the end of the summer, I would go back to Hartford. I kept my apartment there, just in case.'' He opened his mouth to speak, but she cut him off. ''Yes, it was wrong. And stupid. I know it's no excuse, but all I could think about was being with Megan. And then the plan went haywire. I fell in love with you. I didn't want to, but I did. I was terrified of another commitment, but you know what? I got over it. It's too bad I can't say the same for you. You're using what I did as a reason to break us up. You're so afraid of moving forward, you'll grab on to anything to keep you in the past."

She must have hit a nerve, because all the color drained from his face. For a moment she felt the urge to touch him, as she had that night on the balcony after he had kissed her, after he had confused her with his wife. But she held back. She desperately wanted to be in his life, but not as a substitute for what he had lost.

"Are you done *now?*" he asked, his expression tight with strain.

"No. Not yet." She swallowed hard, ready to take the final leap. "At first I believed it was too soon for you to be thinking of someone else, that you were still in love with Cathy, and that would have been okay. I would have accepted it. But I kept thinking about these past few weeks, about all the time we spent together, laughing, talking…making love. Whether or not you admit it, you're in love with me, but you believe it somehow diminishes your feelings for Cathy. You think that by loving me, you'll lose her completely. Well, I have news for you. You're wrong. You don't have to give me the heart you gave Cathy—all you have to do is grow another one. It's a relatively easy procedure—just ask any mother. No matter how many children she has, she grows a new heart for each of them."

"With your track record, you're hardly the person to preach about relationships," he scoffed. "Why is it that whenever a man breaks off with a woman, she accuses him of having a fear of commitment?"

Rachel closed her eyes, as though she could turn off

her frustration by tuning out its source. Adam insisted on playing the opponent. She'd said what she'd set out to say, and he'd refuted her. Now the score was tied and they were in a deadlock.

As if on cue, his cell phone rang, signaling that the match was over.

All Rachel could make out from the conversation was a repetitive "Calm down, sweetheart," sprinkled with the occasional "My God" and one terrifying "Are you sure you're all right?"

"What is it?" she asked, fear knotting inside her.

"That was Megan. The police are at the house. It seems that the Middlewood Minor Mob has struck again."

Rachel recalled the dream she'd had just before the doorbell had awakened her. No matter where she was, no matter how hard she tried to ignore them, she realized that as long as she remained apart from Megan, the dreams would continue to warn her.

She threw a jacket on over her robe and grabbed her purse. "I'm going over there and don't try to stop me. You'd only be wasting your time."

He didn't argue, but she had no illusion about them driving together. He would expect her to return alone.

Chapter Twelve

He knew she was as concerned as he was. He didn't try to stop her from following him to his house, but if she thought this changed things, she had another think coming.

"Rachel!" Megan cried, jumping up from the couch. She hesitated, then asked, "What's *she* doing here?"

"Are you all right?" Rachel asked, but Megan ignored her, refusing to meet her gaze.

Adam glanced around the living room. The curtains from the front windows lay tattered on the floor, next to an overturned stool. A wave of anger washed over him. Taking a few CDs was bad enough, but now these kids had resorted to vandalism. They weren't too bright, either, he concluded. How could they strike again so soon after being arrested? Something else occurred to him. How could they have done all this damage without waking anyone up? And wouldn't Cinnamon have started barking as soon as they had entered the house? Thank God no one had been hurt. "Where are the police?" he asked.

"They left," Paula said. "It wasn't a robbery. I'm sorry, Adam. Evelyn did this. Maybe I should have waited before calling the police, but when I heard a crash, I panicked."

"No, you did the right thing. You didn't know that it wasn't an intruder." He looked at the shredded curtains again, then noticed the broken lamp. "Where is she?" he asked, suddenly very tired. He felt as if the weight of the world had settled on his shoulders.

"I got her calmed down and back to bed. I'm sorry," she repeated. "I should have known she wasn't in her room, but I didn't hear a thing until she fell."

Megan immediately rose to Paula's defense. "Grandma was so quiet, Dad. Like she didn't want anyone to know what she was doing. Paula and I were sleeping, and we didn't hear a sound. Not until Grandma fell and Cinny started barking."

"Are you sure she's all right?" Adam asked. "She didn't have a seizure, did she?"

Paula's mouth was grim. "No, not this time. This time she was lucky."

Lucky, he thought wryly. He slumped down onto the couch and held his head in his hands. He knew that Rachel was watching him from where she stood by the wing chair. Knew she wanted to offer comfort, to both him and Megan. "Why would she cut up the curtains?" he heard her ask. He lifted his head.

"Erika picked them out," Megan said to her father, as though he'd been the one to pose the question. "I don't know why you let her talk you into replacing the old ones in the first place." She turned to Rachel. "My mother liked those curtains," she said pointedly. "Even though they were old. Grandma doesn't like Erika, and she hated these tacky new dishrags."

He supposed it made sense, as much as anything made sense these days. He no longer understood much of what went through his mother's mind, but he knew she disliked Erika. He looked up at Paula. "At least it's over," he said, feigning a relief he didn't feel.

"I don't think so. Look at this place, Adam. The curtains look as though they've been through a paper shredder. And what about the lamp? There could have been a fire. This isn't the first time she's gone on a rampage, and it won't be the last. But there's more."

"You said she was all right," Adam said, fresh anxiety filling him. "What else?"

She showed him her forearm, which was scraped and reddened. "After I helped her up, she attacked me with the scissors. Oh, I'm okay, it's just a surface wound, but it could have been worse. She could have stabbed me. It…it could have happened to Megan."

"You're wrong. She would never hurt anyone. Not on purpose. She was just frightened when you came downstairs."

"No, Dad," Megan said, her voice catching. "When I heard Grandma screaming, I ran downstairs. She and Paula were struggling, just like in the movies. When she saw me, she pulled away from Paula and came after me. She didn't know who I was."

"That's when I managed to take the scissors from her," Paula added.

It was as if Paula was talking about someone else. His mother would never try to harm her, and she certainly wouldn't attack Megan. The woman he knew wouldn't swat a fly, let alone set out to hurt someone she cared about.

Megan looked at him with large, sad eyes. "Grandma didn't mean it. She didn't know what she was doing. You'll see, tomorrow she'll be back to her old self. She just—" She stopped abruptly, a sob taking over her body, tears streaming down her cheeks.

"Megan, let me take you back upstairs," Rachel said softly.

For a moment Adam thought his daughter would relent. Her eyes gleamed with hurt and need, but when Rachel reached for her, Megan pushed her away. "No, stay away from me! You're not part of my family—this is none of your business!"

"Megan, please—"

"Leave me alone. I'm going to my room."

"I'll go with her," Paula said, and followed her upstairs.

A long silence fell. Adam stared out into the hallway, knowing that Rachel was waiting for him to speak. When he didn't, he heard her ask, "What can I do to help?"

Her voice came to him as if through a tunnel. He lay back on the couch and closed his eyes.

Memories of his childhood came flooding back. He thought about how his mother had taught him to skate, spending hours with him at the rink. How every morning she would make him blueberry pancakes, because they were his favorite. How she had taught him to throw a fastball, not because his father couldn't but because he wouldn't spare the time.

How she had run interference between him and his father, when tempers had flared out of control.

His childhood faded into the background, and he remembered how, after he had come back from Berkeley, he had tried to make up for all the years his father had mistreated her.

He thought about what was happening now. How she kept wandering off, how she'd nearly killed Cinnamon, how she'd attacked Paula, how she might have hurt Megan.

He sat quietly, listening to the sounds of the night. Even at this late hour cars were passing by. People were returning to their homes after an evening of...of what? A party? The theater? A late-night movie? It was amazing that outside this house, life went on as usual. Didn't they know that for one remarkable woman, life would never be the same?

The woman he remembered was gone forever.

His mother needed special care, the kind that couldn't be provided at home, but he hadn't been able to see it until now. Hadn't been able to admit it until she had embarked on this spree of destruction, injuring Paula and threatening Megan in the process.

His mind drifted to the night of the opening, when Paula had called him to tell him about the incident with the dryer. Even then, he had refused to see the truth.

But Rachel had known, and she had felt his pain. "What can I do to help?" she'd asked with compassion, just as she'd asked only a moment ago.

Rachel.

He looked up, but she was gone.

She'd felt like a criminal. Like a thief in the night, she had slipped out of the house as insidiously as she had entered their lives.

He didn't even notice when I left, she thought.

After returning to the apartment, she fell into bed,

hoping to catch a few hours of sleep. The morning ahead would be a long one. But her thoughts kept her awake, locking her in a prison of despair.

Before going over to the house, she'd had a shred of hope—hope that her daughter would relent—but now that hope was gone. "You're not part of my family," Megan had said. In the dressing room, when the truth was disclosed, she had spoken from shock, but back at the house her tone had been final.

Rachel felt as if she'd been given a death sentence. No matter what Adam had said, she felt sure that Megan wanted nothing to do with her.

When Rachel finally did fall asleep, her dreams kept her tossing and turning, and when morning came, her head was pounding. The last thing she felt like doing was cleaning the apartment, but she wanted to leave it in the same condition as when she'd moved in. *I should probably empty the refrigerator,* she thought, pouring a glass of juice. She didn't want Adam's friend to come home to a head of wilted lettuce and a carton of sour milk. She put the glass onto the counter and noticed the brightly wrapped package. It was the gift from the cast, forgotten in the confusion of last night. She touched the elegant gold bow, making a mental note to write each member a thank-you note once she got back to Hartford. What a thoughtful, caring bunch of kids they were. Not only had they given her flowers, they had bought her something special to show their appreciation.

Alice's words, *Megan picked it out,* came back to her in a flash, and she tore open the card. "To Rachel, with love," it said. "For the good memories, from the cast." Another card was attached, this one addressed to her in Megan's handwriting. She'd know her daughter's handwriting anywhere—it was uncannily like her own.

"Good memories should have good homes," she read after removing the card from the envelope.

Inside the box was a silver picture frame. She realized it was intended for the photo in the broken frame on her bureau. The photo of her mother pushing her in a stroller. The photo Megan had stared at through the cracked glass.

Rachel felt her eyes moisten as she ran her fingers across the ornamental filigree of the new frame. A question rose in her mind. Had Megan picked out the gift before or after learning the truth? If after, then maybe Adam was right. Maybe Megan was reconsidering.

Then why had she been so cold?

She's confused, Rachel thought. It's too soon for her to reach out to me. Maybe it's true that all she needs is time. Well, she'd soon have all the time she needed. Rachel would be back in Hartford. She fervently hoped that Megan wouldn't wait too long before calling her, but no matter how much time went by, Rachel knew that, for her, it would never be too late.

A daughter needs her mother, all her life.

She removed the photo from the old broken frame and placed it in the new one. It was as if she was giving the picture a fresh start. A second chance, she thought. Everyone deserved a second chance.

She put down the frame and looked over at the phone. Although she hadn't dialed it in years, she remembered the number as though she had called it yesterday. It was ingrained on her soul as clearly as the words on the back of the photo she kept in her purse.

Adam sat at the kitchen table, feeling as grim as Megan looked. "You'll be able to visit her as often as you like," he said. "You don't even need me to take you. It's right on the bus route."

She glared at him from across the table. "Won't you be going? Don't you want to visit your own mother?"

"I meant, if you ever wanted to go alone. It's not as if she'll be that far away."

"Not far away! She might as well be living on the moon!"

Nothing he could say, Adam knew, would make it easier for her to accept that her grandmother would no longer be living with them. He, too, had a hard time accepting it. "I know it's not easy," he started, fighting to keep his emotions contained, "but we're causing her even more harm by keeping her here. She'll get all the care she needs at Belmont Manor."

"You want her to go!" Megan accused. "You're willing to hang on to that broken-down car, but you want to throw away your own mother!"

"No, Megan, you have it all wrong. Sometimes, when it's for the good of the other person, we have to do things we don't like. Sometimes we have no other option."

"What about Rachel? She gave me away, just like you want to give away Grandma. Are you saying that what she did was okay?"

"It's not the same thing," he said quietly. "Rachel had choices. She chose to give you up—" he reached across for her hand "—and we were lucky she did."

Megan pulled her hand away. "Lucky! You always make it sound as if my own mother didn't want me! What if she did? What if she wanted me more than anything in the world? And what about you? You always tell me how much you wanted me, but the truth is, if you and Mom had been able to have your own kids, you never would have adopted me.''

''Megan—''

''What if I turn out to be terrible? Would you stash me in a home, too?''

He felt as if his heart had been wrenched from his chest. ''Megan, you're my daughter. I would never send you away.''

''What about that school in Manhattan? Have you forgotten about that already?''

''That was a mistake,'' Adam admitted. ''At the time I thought it was the best thing for you, but I was wrong.''

''Let me get this straight. You wanted to send me away because you thought it was the best thing for me, but you were wrong. Now you say you would never send me away, just because I'm your daughter. Does that mean you're sending Grandma away because you don't care about her as much as me? And what if you're wrong about her, the way you were wrong about me? What if you realize that making her live in a nursing home is a big mistake?''

Trying to understand Megan's logic was like walking through a maze. ''You're my daughter,'' he repeated, unsure about how to proceed, ''and I always try to do what's best for you. I admit I'm not perfect and I make mistakes, but I promise you that I'll always try to do what's right. As for your grandmother, I just want to do what's best for her—and everyone involved.'' He didn't add that Megan was one of the reasons for his decision. Until last night, if anyone had told him that his mother would become a physical threat to his daughter, he never would have believed it. ''Sometimes it hurts to do what's best. It's time to let go, sweetheart. It's best for Grandma.''

She bit down on her lip. ''I know you're right,'' she said, her voice quivering. ''It's just that it's so hard. First Mom leaves, and now Grandma. But it's true, isn't it? Sometimes you have to let go of someone you love. Sometimes you have no choice.'' She looked up at him as if she wanted to say more, and then, just like that, her eyes hardened and she pushed away from the table. ''If we're going to Doreen's, I'd better get dressed. I suppose I still have to go, right?''

He sighed. ''Doreen is expecting all of us, and I don't want to disappoint her.''

Normally Megan looked forward to Sunday brunch at Doreen's, but this morning she'd told him she wanted to stay home. But he'd been adamant. This would be the last meal they would all share together in Doreen's home, and he wanted Megan to be there.

She'd come up with several excuses why she shouldn't go. She had to walk Cinnamon, even though she'd just walked her. She had to take the garbage out to the curb, even though pickup wasn't until Tuesday. She even tried to convince him that she had reading to do for school, but no summer work had been assigned.

Teenagers, he thought, shaking his head as Megan stomped off to her room. Who could figure them out? Megan wasn't a teen yet, but she sure had all the signs. They must all belong to the same secret club, the National Let's Keep Them Guessing Society.

The Misfits Club, they'd called themselves, according to Rachel. She'd also told him that Megan needed to feel as if she belonged.

He poured another cup of coffee, thinking back to the discussions he and Cathy'd had with Megan regarding the adoption. Tell her she was wanted, the agency had said. Tell her as soon as she's able to understand.

He'd done that and more. He'd told her so many times in a way that made him out to be a prince. A prince who'd rescued her from the evil queen.

He'd made her believe that her natural mother hadn't wanted her. Wasn't that what he'd always believed?

Do you have any idea what it was like, not being able to care for your child, giving her away because you knew it was the only way she would have a chance in this world?

He could hear Rachel's words as clearly as if she were there beside him. Judgmental, she'd called him. Self-righteous.

He was a hypocrite. A judgmental, self-righteous hypocrite.

After cleaning the stove, she washed the kitchen floor. She had other tasks to do, as well, before leaving for Hartford. Leave the key with the landlord—she was paid up until the end of August, but she wasn't expecting a refund. Last-minute packing of odds and ends.

She glanced at the clock on the bureau. It was only a little after ten. If she left within the next half hour, she could be back in Hartford by noon.

What's the rush? she asked herself. It's not as if you have anyone to go back to. It's not as if someone is waiting for you.

She thought about the call she had made, and felt a ray of hope shine through her misery. As soon as she'd heard her mother's voice, Rachel had known that she'd made the right decision in calling. Oh, she wasn't fooling herself. It would take time for her and her mother to rebuild their relationship. And it wouldn't be easy, with Beth living in California. But the process had been started, with one simple call.

Life was too short for grudges. Those had been Megan's words.

After a quick shower, she wiped down the tiles. From the closet next to the bathroom she pulled out the clothes she had set aside last night, a pastel-pink jersey and the denim skirt she had worn to the dress rehearsal.

Megan's locket fell out of the skirt pocket. Megan had asked her to hold it for safekeeping, and Rachel had forgotten to give it back. Why hadn't Megan asked for it after the last performance? Rachel knew how much it meant to her. It was as if Megan was giving Rachel a reason to approach her one last time before leaving for Hartford.

The idea was crazy. What if Rachel had remembered the locket and given it back earlier? How could Megan have known she would forget?

She couldn't have known, but maybe she figured that with everything going on, it was a good possibility. And she'd been right.

But why? Why did Megan feel she needed this extra insurance? If she wanted to talk, why couldn't she just approach Rachel? In the past few days Rachel had tried to talk to her several times, and each time Megan had rebuffed her. Even last night, especially last night, her daughter had made it perfectly clear that she didn't want Rachel in her life.

It didn't make any sense. Unless…

Unless Megan did want Rachel in her life, but was too proud to ask. No, not proud, afraid. Rachel had known about Megan's fear of abandonment, and here Rachel was, about to abandon her daughter again.

Megan needed to feel unconditional love, and not once had Rachel assured her that she wouldn't leave, no matter what, no matter how much Megan kept pushing her away. Rachel had tried to talk to her, but she'd been waiting for the words to come from Megan, waiting for Megan to ask her to stay. And Megan had kept fighting her, testing her, waiting for Rachel to make the commitment.

One last chance. Rachel had been given one last chance. She had to tell Megan she wasn't leaving. Adam had said he wouldn't stand in the way if Megan wanted to see her, but if he had any objections to Rachel remaining in Middlewood, if he tried to interfere, she'd fight him as fiercely as a lioness defending her cub.

Locking the door behind her, she remembered that on Sundays Adam took the family to brunch at Doreen's. I should probably call her, she thought. I should ask her if she'd mind setting an extra place at the table.

"I'm not ready!"

What was keeping her so long? He glanced at his watch. They were already twenty minutes late. "Megan, will you hurry up?"

"Five minutes, Dad!" Megan shouted down from her room.

Ten minutes later she ran down the stairs. "Oops," she said. "I forgot my purse. I'll be back in a minute."

"Megan!" Adam called again from the hallway. "Let's go!"

Evelyn was growing impatient. "We're going to miss the opening act," she complained. "It's not nice to walk into a theater late."

"Megan!" Adam shouted again.

"You don't have to yell," she said, coming down the stairs. "I'm not deaf. Did the mail come yet? I'm expecting my new *Teen Mag*. What if it comes after we're gone?"

Adam rolled his eyes. "It's Sunday. There's no mail."

"I want something to read at Doreen's. I need something to do while you're talking about grown-up things. Unless you want me to watch TV. I'll just run back upstairs and—"

"In the car, Megan. Now."

It was obvious she was purposely trying to delay them. Teenagers, he thought again, as he backed out of the driveway.

As he pulled onto Birch Hill Road, he glanced in the rearview mirror. His mother was sitting quietly in the back seat with Megan, absorbed in the rural scenery. Evelyn turned her head and smiled at his reflection, and he smiled back.

His heart twisted. He knew he had held on too long, causing her unnecessary pain by not being able to provide the care she needed, but he'd never meant to hurt her. What he'd done, holding on, he'd done out of love.

What I did was out of love, not out of malevolence.

Rachel's words came back to him like a shock wave. She'd deceived him and Megan, but as misguided as it was, she had done it out of love. Something else came back to him, and an awakening hit him with such force, he felt himself reeling.

"It's time to let go," he'd told Megan earlier that morning.

Such a simple statement, yet it held so much. Rachel had accused him of living in the past, and she had been right. He'd been holding on too long, closing his eyes to the future, allowing his memories to take over his life.

It was time to let go.

"Dad, what are you doing?" Megan cried, as he spun the car in a U-turn.

"I'm going back," he said. Wrong choice of words,

he thought, grinning. He wasn't going back, he was moving forward. "We're going to Rachel's."

It was after eleven. What if she wasn't there? What if she was already on her way to Hartford? He almost laughed. He'd only known this woman for a little over a month, and he was acting as if...as if what, Wessler?

As if he couldn't bear the thought of spending another minute without her.

He decided to call her on his cell phone to make sure she was at the apartment. If she had already left, he would stop at the community center and dig up her application. On it, he knew, was her address in Hartford. When he'd hired her, he'd believed it was her previous address. Last night she'd told him it was current.

He pulled over onto the shoulder and took out his phone. One ring, then two. Three. Seven.

Well, that settled it. They were going to Hartford. But when he shifted into gear and stepped on the gas, Ethel refused to budge.

Was that Ethel? How many other classic Chrysler DeSotos could there be in this town?

She glanced at the car on the left shoulder, then made a quick U-turn and parked behind Adam's car.

"Having trouble?" she asked, climbing out of the driver's seat.

She was reminded of when they first met. Only now, instead of holding a hammer, he carried a wrench. Instead of a dirt-smudged suit, he wore a Giants T-shirt and snug faded jeans, and both were stained with grease.

He lifted his head from under the hood. "Rachel! I can't believe you're here!"

"Oh, I'm here all right, and I'm planning to stay. And

don't try to talk me out of it, because I've made up my mind.''

"I just wanted to say—"

"Save it," she said, using the same tone he'd taken when he'd spoken the same words last night. "Right now I need to speak to Megan. I'll deal with you later."

He stood by the car, giving her a strange crooked smile, his arms crossed over his chest. She didn't know what was going through his head, but at least he had the good sense not to stop her from going to Megan. She was determined to resolve this thing with her daughter and she wasn't about to let anything or anyone, not even the pompous and fastidious Adam Wessler, stand in her way.

Megan jumped out of the car. "I knew you would come, I just knew it! I waited at the house for as long as I could, but then—" As if a barrier had been dropped between them, she stopped abruptly and looked away.

Rachel reached into her pocket and took out the locket. "I wanted to get this back to you right away. I know how much you love it. I was on my way to your house when I remembered that you would be going to Doreen's for brunch."

"I guess you wanted to drop it off before you left for Hartford."

"Leave for Hartford?" Rachel repeated, feigning surprise. "What are you talking about? Oh, I admit I considered going back when I thought you didn't want me to stay, but I decided that no matter how much of a fuss you make, no matter how much you kick and scream, you're stuck with me. Not even a bulldozer could make me move away."

Apparently she had said just the right thing, because her daughter beamed. "Or even a tow truck," Megan said, giggling. "Look, Grandma! Rachel brought back my necklace."

Evelyn stuck out her hand and waved through the open window. "She's a good girl. Looks just like her mother. Ask her to come to brunch with us."

"Will you, Rachel? Except we might all have to go in your car. I don't know if Dad'll ever gets this heap back on the road."

Megan looked so eager, so happy to see her. Rachel wanted to hug her, and she did. "I love you, Megan," she said. "Forever and ever. Mother and daughter, me and my darling princess."

"She's as pretty as a princess," Evelyn said.

Megan glanced at her father, then back at Rachel. "Say you'll come with us to Doreen's, Rachel. Please? It's a family meal, and I want you to sit next to me. Dad, make her say yes!"

"Am I allowed to talk now?" Adam asked.

Rachel looked back at him. "I don't want to intrude. Just because I'm staying in Middlewood, doesn't mean you have to—"

"Didn't you hear what Megan said?" he interrupted, still wearing that silly, crooked grin. "She said it was a family meal, and you're family, Rachel."

For a moment Rachel felt too stunned to speak, and then gratitude took over. "Thank you, Adam. Thank you for allowing me to be a part of my daughter's life."

"I wasn't just talking about *her* life," he said softly. "Uh, Megan, I think Grandma is getting bored. Can you sit with her in the car?"

"She's busy looking at the trees. I want to stay out here with—" A wide grin spread across her face. "You're right. She does look a little bored. You know what they say, once you've seen one birch tree, you've seen them all,'' she joked, and climbed back into the car.

He turned back to Rachel. "Do you believe in fate?"

"Wh-what?"

"Fate. As in destiny. After what you said about your dreams, I would think you'd know all about that mystical stuff."

"I guess so," she said, unsure of where the conversation was headed.

"I was on my way to Doreen's house, when I decided to turn around. I wanted to talk to you and I wanted to do it in person. And here you are. If that's not fate, what is?"

Her heart took a leap. Did he want to discuss her relationship with Megan—or with him? "You wanted to talk to me? Why?"

"To tell you that I've been a jackass. To tell you that I don't want you to go. To tell you that I don't want to spend another minute without you."

These were the words she'd been waiting for, and now that he had said them, she didn't know how to respond. She felt as if she were dreaming. But unlike her dreams of the past, this one was filled with promise. "You love me," she said simply, as though saying the words aloud could make the dream come true.

"Yes, Rachel, I love you," he said, flashing her another crooked smile, "but I have to admit, I like hearing you say it. Like last night, when you told me I was in love with you. I figured you had to be telling the truth, since everything else you said made sense. Well, almost everything."

She felt her body tense. "You mean my dreams?"

"I'm still not convinced they meant anything, but I have no doubt that you believe they did. And anyway, what do I know about all that stuff? Look what happened today.''

"Fate," she said with trepidation, as though afraid to tempt it. Everything she'd ever wanted was right here in front of her. "You're telling me that it was because of fate that I found you stranded on the road."

"If I hadn't decided to swerve around, if I hadn't pulled onto the shoulder, if Ethel hadn't decided to take a long nap, you wouldn't have seen my car. You would have missed me."

"Your logic is faulty. I would have met you at Doreen's."

"No, I would have been halfway to Hartford. And you, Ms. Hartwell, would be sitting at Doreen's table, trying to pretend you weren't miserable. Not about her cooking, mind you. She always makes a great spread, which you'll soon find out. I want you to come with us today, and for every Sunday after. But I have to warn you," he said, drawing her close and whispering in her ear, "Sunday brunch is not all I have planned."

"Why don't you kiss her already!" Evelyn called from the back seat.

"Puh-leeze, Grandma!" Megan said. "Give them a little privacy."

Rachel laughed. "So what else do you have in mind, hotshot?"

His expression stilled. "The rest of our lives," he said, wrapping his arms around her, and to the applause of their two onlookers sealed the pledge with his kiss.

CURTAIN CALL

Epilogue

It was a funny thing about Ethel, Rachel thought, waving at the well-wishers gathered outside the house. Adam's classic DeSoto was running just fine these days. It hadn't conked out once since that August Sunday on Birch Hill Road.

Happy faces smiled back at them as Adam held open the door and she climbed into the front seat. Her mother stood next to Megan, her arm around her granddaughter's shoulders. She would be staying with Megan while Rachel and Adam were in Vermont on their honeymoon. Adam had some kind of delusion about tearing down the slopes on a snowboard, but Rachel had other plans for him. She had a few winter fantasies of her own.

The snow on the front lawn sparkled in the January

sunshine. On the front porch, Paula was holding Evelyn's mittened hand. She had taken a day off from her new job as a baby nurse to attend the wedding, and had sat with Evelyn in the chapel during the ceremony. She would be driving her back to Belmont Manor after all the guests had gone.

Erika had graciously declined Rachel's invitation. Recently relocated to New York City, she had sent a punch bowl in lieu of her presence.

With Megan as maid of honor, the wedding had been perfect, a wonderful start to a new life. After the ceremony, friends and family had gathered at the house for a brunch reception.

Filled with contentment, Rachel settled back in her seat as Adam slid behind the wheel. "Ready to hit the slopes?" her new husband asked, leaning over to kiss her before starting the car.

"Ready and willing," she bantered back, and turned around for one last look at the happy group in front of the house.

And then she saw her.

A tall, slender woman in a green, flowing gown emerged from the shadows beneath the porch roof. At her throat a prism of colors glittered like diamonds, and for a moment Rachel thought she saw a heart-shaped pendant. The woman smiled, and then, as quickly as she had appeared, vanished in a shimmer of bright winter light.

"So, *Ms.* Wessler, how do you feel about our future so far?" Adam asked as he pulled away from the curb.

There was only one answer. "It's a dream come true."

* * * * *